My Invisible Wings

A Collection of Short Stories for Women by a Woman

AAR AAR

iUniverse, Inc.
New York   Bloomington

Copyright © 2010 by aar aar

All rights reserved. No part of this book may be used or reproduced by any means, graphic, electronic, or mechanical, including photocopying, recording, taping or by any information storage retrieval system without the written permission of the publisher except in the case of brief quotations embodied in critical articles and reviews.

Copyrighted by: Canadian Intellectual Property Office on October 26, 2007

iUniverse books may be ordered through booksellers or by contacting:

iUniverse
1663 Liberty Drive
Bloomington, IN 47403
www.iuniverse.com
1-800-Authors (1-800-288-4677)

Because of the dynamic nature of the Internet, any Web addresses or links contained in this book may have changed since publication and may no longer be valid. The views expressed in this work are solely those of the author and do not necessarily reflect the views of the publisher, and the publisher hereby disclaims any responsibility for them.

ISBN: 978-1-4401-9668-3 (sc)
ISBN: 978-1-4401-9670-6 (hc)
ISBN: 978-1-4401-9669-0 (ebook)

Printed in the United States of America

iUniverse rev. date: 02/16/2010

Foreword By Salman Ahmed of Asia's number one rock band, Junoon.

Salman's band, Junoon, is popular all over the globe. He is a medical doctor who chose music as a peace vehicle. Salman is a UN goodwill ambassador for HIV/AIDS, and he is working towards spreading awareness about HIV in South Asia. He is also actively working towards bringing peace between India and Pakistan. Salman has worked with world renowned artists including Annie Lennox, Sarah McLachlan, and Dave Stewart.

In the summer of 1995, Ranga Rajah first interviewed me at the Hyatt regency in Dubai for *Gulf Today*. Even then, I saw a sparkle in her eye that went beyond the cut and dry of many modern journalists. I saw in her a hunger to tell stories that illuminate the universal humanity of our world with all its beauty, laughter, and pain.

Writing this foreword for Ranga's new book gives me immense joy. I see her writing as something every woman will be able to relate to. It speaks of the trials and triumphs women endure on their journeys. I wish her infinite abundance and success with this book, and I look forward to reading many more in the future.

Onwards on the journey of Light,
Salman

They supported and encouraged me to write…

Salman Ahmed is a friend, and a true one at that. He very graciously took time out of his busy schedule and agreed to write a foreword for this book. It is an honor for me, an unknown writer, to have his name in my book.

I have known Salman for almost a decade now. All I can say is he deserves all the success he has earned. He is a true champion and is very hardworking. He is an achiever who is first and foremost a great human being with a great passion. I would like to thank Salman for his friendship, encouragement, and inspiration.

Karen: Never would I have imagined publishing my tales if it weren't for your support. The words are mine, but the spirit and encouragement is all yours.

Raghu, for listening to all my stories and feeling the emotions with me. Thank you so very much.

Natarajan: How do I define your friendship? You are a true friend.

Pradeep, my boss, an honest friend: You really rock! Thank you for keeping me employed all through my journey as a writer and for having faith in my tales. I owe my life in Canada to you and your company.

Pradeep, you are someone very special, because people have seen me flying always and flying high. What they have missed are the invisible threads that held my wings.

Joseph Karaparambil, my illustrator: Thank you for translating my thoughts into neat sketches and illustrations.

Author's Note

How does a writer narrate tales? I have a very vague idea myself. I started writing because I love words. I try and express myself as clearly as I can with their help. Words have lent me all the support they could in this journey of mine. I am planning to keep this support ongoing as long as I can. Words, I feel, will stay with me no matter what. They might fail me at times, like so many instances when I was speechless, because being a writer, I can never speak very well; I express my angst, my happiness, and all my abstract thoughts through words.

In my narrations I wanted to talk about the strength of women. She could be eighty years old or eight years old, she can be any age or generation; my women are people who endure happiness and sorrow and emerge stronger.

I owe this book to my son, Nesah, because he is my inspiration in life to live it, to fight, and to make the most of it.

I also owe it to Rajah, for giving me all possible opportunities to experience and live life. With him, I have truly tested and experienced life.

Mississauga has been my home for over six years now. I grew up in the suburbs of Bombay; traveling by local trains to go to school, to university, and later to work was something I enjoyed. I enjoyed train travel because it gave me time to read, write, and dream. I worked with the *Times of India* in Bombay and later in Bangalore. I also worked for *Gulf Today* and freelanced for *Gulf News* in the UAE. Currently I am working in a restaurant as a server/manager.

Chapter 1

Day: Maya, wake up. The milkman is ringing the doorbell, and I'm guessing the newspaper is here too.

Maya: Puggu, I've just lost my job. I don't want to face the milkman. I have no money. Life isn't worth living.

Day: I know from your tone that you're about to go into self-pity and complaint. Anyway, Rituka, Arundhati's daughter, is back from wherever she went so many years ago. At least she came home for her mother's funeral.

Maya: What's the story behind Arundhati and her many men? She's eighty years old, and I hear she's led a pretty colorful life.

Day: Don't talk about things you don't understand. Let me tell you briefly about Arundhati's life. She made sure her family was settled and decided that she didn't want to be a burden on anyone. Everyone, including her son Kedar and his wife and kids, and Surendra, her husband, treated her like a queen, but she chose to stay in the shelter during the last decade and a half of her life. She said she had seen and lived life to its fullest.

Maya: Okay, tell me her story.

Readings from Arundhati's Diary

It is Arundhati's funeral, and there are three men and a young lady standing in different corners. How was Arundhati related to all these men? One is her husband, one is her son, and one is the man who loved her for all that she was, in a relationship that could never be described. The young lady is her estranged daughter. Arundhati died in a shelter for women. She was eighty years old at the time of her death.

Her Son Kedar is thinking: 'I wish I had more time with her. I know the troubles she has gone through to raise me and make a man out of me. She always wanted me to carve a niche for myself and be a good student. She was willing to let me make mistakes, but she asked me to learn and not repeat those mistakes. How many times she supported me…I've lost count. My first brawl, the night I came home drunk after my first party as a teenager. I didn't know how to handle my drinks. She lovingly told me how to enjoy a drink and not get drunk. She advised me to drink when I'm celebrating or happy, not when I'm down and out or sad. Ma also taught me how to respect women, and she gently told me the subtle differences between love, infatuation and lust.

According to her, love is that momentary attraction that we take to the next level by working at relationships. She always wanted me to take my responsibilities seriously. Her constant fear was that I might fail at being a responsible family man. She taught me to value things in life. She taught me how to save ten percent of every dollar I earn. Ma, came from a highly scattered family with no bonding. Her father died when she was quite young. She did all that she could to keep me happy, to help me grow into a strong individual mentally, physically, and emotionally. By the grace of god and her blessings I have a family and I take good care of them. My wife loves me and often thanked my mother for raising me well.

I wish I could get one warm assuring hug out of her. I miss her now. I miss her now that she is no more. I am going to miss her warm kisses on my forehead and my cheek, and her hands rubbing my forehead after she finished her prayers and before she left home for work. "My mother, I could use one last smile from you to tell me everything will be fine."

Kedar's thoughts were interrupted by the priest, who was explaining some formalities about Arundhati's cremation. Kedar led the priest to where his father was standing, lost in thoughts of Arundhati.

Surendra, Arundhati's husband, remembered her as a sharp-tongued person. He remembered how, after their marriage, he had to deal with a person who wasn't in touch with reality and not worldly wise at all. All she could think of was having a family and wanting him around her and the children. There's nothing wrong with this sentiment, but for Surendra, life was a little more than just family dinners and outings. For him it was the burning ambition to make money. Arundhati had come to him with nothing but a few thousand rupees that lasted for a little over two months after their marriage. They both had to look for jobs, and life was difficult for them. Arundhati had romantic notions about not taking help from anybody but working hard to make a life and build family together.

To Surendra, this idea was just a silly romantic notion. After Kedar was born, Surendra decided to take a chance in this big world, so he went from one country to another and finally settled in London. Arundhati followed him. Surendra was losing money in his business, and after buying a home in London, he moved to Paris to try his hand at another business. He traveled to London every two weeks to see Kedar and Arundhati.

Today, standing here, he realised that now he had no place to go and see her, after all these years when he had hardly managed to spend any time with her. Arundhati had talked about wanting to go on vacations as a family, even for weekends, but they never could make it as a family. Some commitment or other kept Surendra from being with them on vacation.

Vacation with family for Arundhati remained a dream, but then, most of her dreams remained just dreams. What was she thinking now? Was she still dreaming of family? Dinners, poojas, festivals, and maybe picnics and vacations. Is she even capable of thinking or dreaming in the state she's in now? Surendra wondered and sighed heavily, struggling to look at his wife's face as she lay dead.

Preetam only knew her as a lady who was ambitious and would kill to get things done at her job. She was fierce, and she got what she wanted. In his opinion, Arundhati was a model worker, not too demanding of others but highly demanding of herself. She set goals and achieved them, even if it meant juggling her domestic life, with its strife and tension from her teenagers. She balanced her home and work beautifully. When did she sleep? Preetam wondered. She started work early and finished well after midnight and didn't hesitate to take calls any time of the day.

Preetam was a lawyer, and she assisted him. They were married to their jobs and dreamed big. She worked for over six years in his company and gave it all she had, but misunderstandings between them caused rifts. They both were strong-minded, and neither was willing to compromise. He loved her, and she loved him, but in a different way. Like so many lives she touched, she touched his life as well. He wished they had met 35 years earlier; he thought their lives would have been different. But Arundhati didn't think so. How different would their lives have been, he wondered. He looked at Arundhati's daughter standing in the corner of the room.

Rituka and Arundhati didn't understand one another; they couldn't be close. Rituka felt there was no need for marriage, that to dream of creating a family was a waste. She often cited Arundhati's failure to create a close family as an example. Drugs, music, partying, and painting were Rituka's passions, and she thought her mother should let her follow her heart. She wanted no boundaries. Uncertainty and fear of commitment about everything in her life, including men, was Rituka's trademark. She missed having a father figure more than Kedar did. She went after men looking for assurance, and Rituka remembered her mother lecturing her on how to be self-assured and not be a clinging vine.

But Rituka could never shake off her low self-esteem. She became addicted to drugs, and later to isolation and to books. Nothing was consistent in her life; she wandered aimlessly, and then she left home to join a cult in the Americas. She never got in touch with her family except to call either Surendra or Arundhati once a year to let them know that she was alive and seeking something she couldn't identify. Rituka remembered the day she called Arundhati and cursed her for bringing her into this world, so uncaring and full of hypocrites. She said she was so depressed that she wanted to kill herself or kill everybody else. She blamed Arundhati for not being around when a daughter needed her mother most. If Rituka was clueless, she said, it was because Arundhati was so involved with her career and the money it brought in. After Rituka had vented for more than forty minutes, the phone went dead. Her mother had hung up.

This incident had happened eight years before. Rituka had served her sentence for five years at a prison and another three years at a rehab centre. It was by chance that she had called her mother and Kedar answered the phone. He told her about Arundhati's whereabouts. Apparently she had left their home to live in a shelter for women where she had been volunteering for many years. It was her favorite place, he said.

Rituka wanted to show her new self to her mother. She had become wiser. and now she understood Arundhati and her pain a little better. She wanted to reach out to her mother, take her to movies and drive-in eateries that Arundhati liked. Sometimes when Kedar or Rituka needed something from Arundhati, they made plans for such outings, and every time they managed to fool Arundhati and get what they wanted.

Rituka arrived five days after she called home, and by then it was too late. Arundhati had died the previous evening. Rituka wanted just one chance to tell Arundhati that she didn't blame her any more. As a woman she wanted to salute her mother for trying her best at everything, including managing her home, kids, job, and self. In her world of endless possibilities, Rituka desired one magical moment with her mother. She wanted one moment to share a look that would say, 'I know now what it is to be a woman.'

After the funeral, Kedar and Rituka read Arundhati's diary.

For Kedar

Today is a beautiful day. I am happy Kedar has begun to understand the value of time, money, and people. I wanted that for him. I liked the way he tried to help that old man in his wheelchair. Something about Kedar's gesture told me he wanted to reach out to the old man from the bottom of his heart. I never knew Kedar would make a good parent, but he is a very good parent. I have managed to instill correct values in him. I am proud that he and his wife chose to adopt Lata instead of having their own child. It does not matter where I am, alive or in spirit, I will always be there with you. my son.

Kedar knew his mother would always be there, filling his life with reassurance.

After flipping a few pages, they found something for Rituka.

My Invisible Wings 7

For Rituka

I know it must be difficult out there for my daughter. Life as a woman is complex. So many roles to play, and so much social conditioning to break free from. I have heard that she is supporting herself by working as an escort. Well, I am sure that job requires a lot of hard work as well. No matter what, I will not judge my daughter, or any woman for that matter. Rituka will find her bearings, I am sure of that. God knows I tried to guide the girl. But she had to find herself— she always wanted to do that right from the time she was three or four. Always daydreaming and planning to change the world. There was always some deep, fierce dormant anger in her. She is a sensitive soul, my daughter, I know you will emerge strong and self-assured. You will go on to inspire people with your honesty and deep understanding of the human psyche.

Rituka shed a tear that didn't relieve the pain deep in her heart that she felt would stay with her forever.

They found a page with their father's name on it. They tore it out and handed it to Surendra.

For Surendra

I knew the day I married Surendra that I would have to be the responsible one and raise the family. Surendra will never realize he is the weaker one in this partnership. It is okay, he is my partner. Marriage is not just partying and vacations, it is also holding your partner at times when he is about to fall. Some partners just like to be comforted. Surendra needs that all the time. I have no dreams ... I realize I am incapable of dreaming. I am far too realistic and practical to believe, to live in a dream world. Unlike Surendra, I take each day as it comes, and life becomes easy for me. Yes, my son, my daughter (wherever she is) and Surendra are the few people I derive my strength from. I want peace and happiness for Surendra. I want him to find his corner of life, the corner, that piece of life that has been eluding him. He thought he had found it in me, but he realised later that it was not in me. Poor Surendra, never one to break anybody's heart, never mentioned it. He somehow kept himself occupied and managed to keep moving in life. I wish him happiness.

Surendra wished that Arundhati could come alive for just a few minutes… just a few minutes …

Rituka went looking for Preetam. She found his office and gave him his pages, which Kedar wouldn't do.

For Preetam

If only Preetam knew the kind of person I am. I am nothing like what he thinks. His idea of a partner is someone like me—strong, independent, ambitious, a go-getter. And he also thinks of me as carefree or a person who doesn't give a damn about others. I am none of these. These are all façades I put on when I get to the office. I need to be this and a little more; it's my professional persona. Once I take off that make-up, I'm a loser, a person who feels lonely and left out by people she loves. I need people to pamper me, to assure me that they will be by my side when I am alone. I'm scared of dying alone or in penury. I am a person who wants to keep a home, tend to children, go to movies and have a good laugh. Yes, I love my wine too. I would love to be wined and dined and would be thrilled to get some flowers. Preetam loves my strong person façade. If he found me crying and feeling devastated because of an inability to cope with loneliness, he would never say, I wish I had met you 35 years ago.

Rituka and Kedar together read this page from their mother's diary, and then Rituka tore it out and kept it for herself.

I am just as much a woman as any other woman in this world, just the kind Preetam and other men find irritating. To Preetam and other men who fall for just one aspect of any woman, I would like to tell you, we have as many shades as a chameleon, as many layers as an onion. At each time and each phase of our lives, we look different. Men create an impression of us in their minds and want us to stay in that frame, just as they imagine. We happen to show a side they don't know, they always find it difficult to accept. Men, I've figured out, are not capable of handling different sides of a woman. No offence intended, but men think in a much more straightforward fashion than women.

Here's a little secret: It isn't just men who wonder about us women. We take an entire lifetime to find ourselves. Yes, one thing is certain, no matter how we express ourselves to the men in our lives, we're all looking for appreciation and support. We definitely speak the same language, all of us. Remember men, you will be surprised to find shades of Azra in Rima, shades of Rima in Sunita and Sonia, but one thing is for sure, men (including my son and others) help shape and carve our personalities. As women, all we need is confidence in ourselves and to make sure we don't get pulled in different directions. We are far stronger and far more powerful than we ever give ourselves credit for, and that's precisely why we don't get the credit we deserve.

Chapter 2

Maya has managed to get a job as a customer service representative. She doesn't like it much, but she's been trying to make it to work for almost a week now.

Day: Maya, it's 8:00. Get up. What are you going to do today?

Maya: I feel lazy. I don't feel like cooking, and I don't feel like going to work. Oh, close the blinds, the sunlight hurts my eyes.

Day: So why did you stay awake till 4:00 sipping wine and watching Hrithik Roshan dance?

Maya: What shall I do, Puggu? I have such a miserable life. I want a piece of good life too.

Day: Okay, you want good things. How do you plan to make that possible? You can't just want it and have it, Maya, you need to work for it.

Maya: I tried my hand at every job I could get. Puggu, what do you really know about me? All you can see is this self, this middle-aged, tired, frustrated, lonely self. And miserable. Don't forget miserable!

Day: Don't be so hard on yourself. Get out of bed and make a cup of hot golden liquid to cheer you up.

Maya: What's got into you? What golden liquid are you talking about? I only drink white wine.

Day: (Laughing) Now, now, don't get any ideas. I was talking about tea.

Maya: Oh that. Yes, I better get that cup of cheer. My head hurts and I have a long day ahead of me. It might be pay day today, and I need to pay bills and send Richu's tuition fees. Hey, I can see split ends on my hair. I have to get a haircut, and I'll get her to massage my scalp.

Day: My dear queen, if you take time off from daydreaming, you might be able to get a lot of things done.

Maya: Queen? (She chuckles) We women are treated like queens only when we demand to be. If we give men an inch, they'll bury us alive. But wait, I have to remember I'm trying to learn. I'll tell stories that I've heard, so listen. I'll tell you stories, in chapters, one every day or so. Are you willing to listen, and then we'll talk about what to do with my life?

Day: Okay—done.

Maya: Here's my first tale: Bhanu's story, told by herself.

And Then I Found Life …

I heard harsh words used liberally when I was a kid, because Mother was always in a foul mood, swearing at older siblings. She was drowned in problems of day-to-day survival, especially money, trying to put food on the table, to pay bills.

I was brought up by a single mother is an expression I always debate with myself. Father was a bum who always managed to live life king-sized without making any attempt to earn a decent living to support his family.

I was somewhere in the middle, the sixth or fifth child of twelve siblings. Hand-me-downs were a problem, since my older sister got clothes from charitable rich people. Bags of clothes would come every three months—even undergarments. The clothes smelled of stale perfumes. Sometimes I even wore hand-me–downs from those bags that siblings already had worn.

School fees were always a problem. I remember walking back home early from school for not paying fees for more than three months.

Although I was an above average student, I used to dread school for plenty of reasons besides not being able to pay school fees. I never had a pencil box, a lunch box, or even books. I was scared to ask for color pencils and paper. Additional study materials or extra tuition requests never crossed my mind.

My sister used to take me on rounds to rich people's homes and introduce us (my siblings and me) as people she knew from slums. She didn't want to introduce us as poor relatives. This was because my older sister had introduced herself as a social worker, and she had gained entry into their world because of that tag. So once a month we went begging for tuition fees from affluent people. The list included film personalities, industrialists, and socialites. When enough money was collected, she used half for her expenses, a part was given to us, and a little would go to my mother for household expenses. We were also encouraged to use our share for household expenses instead of school fees. Being young, I never realized we were misusing money meant for education.

A famous filmmaker who was renovating his home had a roomful of stuff to give away. There were books, color pencils, clothes, handbags, puzzles, building blocks, and other goodies piled up in that huge room. I can still remember how bright the room looked, filled to the corners with sunlight. After admiring the collection for a while, I gathered as much as I could. There were books, including Enid Blyton's fairy tales and Tin Tin comics. There were color pencils and crayons from America.

I lost myself in those books and colors. With my block collection, I could build a farm house facing a multistory building. How I cried when I lost a few pieces because of space constraints. At home, I never had a place to call my own, not even a corner. I had a shelf in a cupboard used by all seven of us. Maybe there were fifteen of us.

When my sister got married, her husband and children also came to that tiny house. Then my share of clothes, always few, became even smaller. The best were put aside for my sister's kids. I do remember reading and forgetting any existence outside books. Nothing else mattered to me then—not food, not good clothes, not even school at times. My world was buried between pages and in chapters of books. When I finished reading the books I had brought from the film personality's home, I would go to a secondhand bookstore and buy illustrated books for cheap prices.

I often stayed home from school because of my fears about being sent home for not paying fees. Sometimes I was at home because I hadn't done my homework due to various reasons such as no books or reference material, no paper, or no supplies such as a compass to measure angles. I ran errands on those days. On days when there was no money, I had to run to the pawn shop to pawn gold or silver jewelry, copper or steel vessels, anything that was available, followed by shopping for essentials, especially food. Mother would cook, but my errands didn't ensure a meal for me. For some reason I never felt hungry. I was too engrossed in my books, in my world filled with words and fantasies. I had no friends, and home was loveless. I was hungry for food, love, guidance, and everything else. My unfortunate childhood provided shelter, but that shelter never protected me from fear, insecurity, and pain.

I remember one day when I wanted to reread a certain spooky tale. I hunted high and low for that book, but it seemed to have vanished. Many more books also went missing. They were part of me, my collection. Later on I realized that my books were going to the recycling store, where my brother sold them and got money for his cigarettes. How I cried and cursed him. This was competition at the lowest level—a struggle to hold onto any bit belonging to me.

I did have some good times. I loved popular songs. I had a musical sense, catching the rhythm quickly. I tried my hand at writing, and realized I could pen a few expressions that made sense, but I never planned for the future. I didn't nurture any ambition because I didn't know how, and I didn't miss it.

I managed to get my secondary school cleared and went to high school. In school I had managed to win dance competitions, and I was a runner-up in an essay competition. The money situation was the same, but I was a teenager now and started tutoring other students. I made a few friends; we went to restaurants and I tasted good food. I developed an appreciation for food, and life was beginning to make some sense. I remember my mother taking me to a shop where they sold cotton fabric, and I chose red and green fabric and made a dress for myself. I loved wearing my dresses to school.

A vendor named Pushpa used to bring us things: fabric, pickles, snacks. Mother used to buy, but we never had any money to pay her dues. She was a Hindu who had come to India from Pakistan, a very hardworking lady. I loved her determination and courage.

She lived in a refugee camp and raised five children. She educated them all. I lost track of her after I left home. I wonder whatever happened to her.

An old lady named Ajji used to bring us milk, butter, and vegetables from her farm. She traveled three hours to bring us our supplies every week. Mother never had any money to pay her either. Mother's defense was either speaking extra humbly or shouting aggressively. I owe my childhood to these two patrons, as well as all the rich people who were generous, giving us hand-me-downs, books, and money.

I connect food and eating with Pushpa and Ajji. I remember one day in particular that Ajji invited me and my mother to stay at her farm. How did she have such a big heart that she invited the people who owed her money? Believe it or not, we walked for forty-five minutes through woods to a river or stream and took a ferry for about a half-hour to reach her village. Her home was a mud house with cows and buffaloes in the shed. She had a storeroom, a few more rooms, and a kitchen where she cooked on a charcoal stove. She cooked us a simple meal of chicken and bread. It tasted delicious, a different kind of delicious, so that the memory of the taste lingers even after many years. After dinner, in a corner in a small room, we were given a brass water pitcher and a few handmade quilts to make ourselves comfortable.

We woke up just before dawn to the sound of buffalo being milked. I stepped out to get a feel of the dawn and found that everyone was busy except us. I needed to go to the bathroom as well. Ajji pointed me towards the bushes and gave me a tumbler of water. There were no bathrooms or even partitions; it was all out in the open. We had to squat. After I finished my morning bowel routine, I returned to the backyard and found another bucket of warm water and a clean towel laid on a wooden platform with charcoal and burnt wood ash to brush my teeth. After brushing our teeth, we were directed to a cubicle that was a nine-yard sari made into a cotton screen. In the cubicle, we took our baths.

Breakfast was tea and rusk, and then we walked for a half-hour to visit her daughter-in-law's village. We had lunch there, and then Mother and I returned home. I don't remember how we got back, but I do remember that we didn't take the ferry.

Why is this trip so memorable? I think I longed for the routine these people had in their lives. They were poor, like us, but my home was always in a state of chaos. I don't remember a moment when I was peaceful or calm. Our lane had a water connection, but the water was limited to a few hours, and some days the taps went dry for no reason. When there was a water shortage, I had to rush with a bundle of clothes to any nearby water source. It might be a well where I had to draw water for us to bathe and wash.

If not the well, I had to go to a railway colony where they had running water with high pressure 24/7. But at the colony we were at the mercy of their schedule for families, so we had to look for other sources.

I was responsible for most of the housework, and when I was older it became my duty to cook every day, to clean, and to hand wash clothes for eighteen people. The laundry included heavy bedsheets, dirty undergarments, you name it, I had to wash it, even when I went to high school every day. Housework was never-ending. With a mother who had lost all her energy giving birth to twelve children, it was very rough for me. My mother neither encouraged nor discouraged anything, whether it was good or bad, evil or virtuous, fair or unfair. She was set in a neutral mode. Nothing affected her. Even when my sister started raising her family in our small house, Mother didn't speak out. It suited her to have a daughter who brought in some money working at odd jobs. My sister's husband and five children were a permanent fixture. Later on, she separated from her husband.

My brothers were turning out to be bums. Father, useless as usual, got married to another woman and brought her home as well. A sister of mine, after requesting parents to look out for a groom, decided to elope with a guy without leaving any address. Another sister had a job and gave part of her salary to the family. One sister was adopted by a rich distant relative. We were a family of almost twenty people living in a 20 ft. by 30 ft. house. Twenty-five dollars a month was all we had for family income. I always wanted a corner of my own, and I looked for private time to read, dream, write, and fantasize about prince charming.

Even late at night, my sister who pretended to be a social worker would walk in after finishing her odd jobs, such as singing in a chorus or acting as an extra in a movie, and ask me to make her fresh bread and garlic sauce. She always insisted on tea with her meal.

I remember rushing out to bring water in huge pots, balancing one on my hip and the other one on my head, as late as 12:30 a.m. My sister or my mother would find out there would be a water shortage the next day, so I would run to the nearby railway canteen. I knew the railway platform canteen contractor waited until 2:00 a.m. for the last local train before closing shop for two hours, and sometimes I would collect water at that time. I used to enjoy the calmness and stillness of the night, and I would sing to myself.

Home was just a three-minute walk from the station. There was a mahua tree on the way. and people spread tales that it was haunted. My heart always skipped a beat when I passed that tree. Mahua is a type of flower used by local breweries to brew cheap liquor. When I knew this round would be the last one before I filled that 70-liter drum at home with water, I would take it easy and look around for the ice & candy man's cart. He used to cover his cart with plastic covers and in a jute sack, covered with saw dust to protect his ice blocks from melting. I used to love to feel the coolness against my hand.

The ice cart parked beneath a banyan tree next to the railway tracks, where a gate went down when trains came. The cart and the mahua and banyan trees were to my right as I walked, and on my left was a restaurant that sold nonvegetarian items. Next to it was a grocer who was licensed to distribute our monthly ration of subsidized rice, oil, lentils, cream of wheat, sugar, and wheat, followed by a vegetarian restaurant, a barber shop where I went to get my hair trimmed once in a while. Girls went to barbers, not beauty shops, in those days. There was a dairy, a laundry and dry cleaner who washed and ironed clothes, a flour mill that pounded wheat to flour for fresh rotis and bread.

At the end of the row, there was a vegetable shop that was also a quack clinic. This gentleman had cured me of a rash and other ailments. He was a savior for people who didn't have money for doctors and medicines. He practiced country medicine and distributed it free.

When I reached this spot, I could see the red-tiled roof of my home. I dreaded going inside, for my time alone would be over, and housework or some other demand would suck me in. With all this, I was still in high school, and I had about ten students coming to me for after-school help. I taught them languages and science and managed to make about $10, paid to me by some students and I also gave free tuitions to some. Well, I knew what it is to be poor and not get support to study.

I began to have a life at school, but I dreaded Saturdays and Sundays at home. I wanted to escape, but where? I found places to hang out at markets bustling with activity of vendors and busy restaurants.

I chose a music shop. I loved collecting records and later cassettes. Nothing could beat my love for radio—it was number one. Music took me to faraway lands in the imaginary world I created for myself. I danced all the time.

I kept myself as busy as I could. I had one friend, a girl named Jamuna. My family worked in her family's house as domestic help. We were in the same class. She was a bright student and we decided to hang out together. I guess her mother felt I was a bad influence on her daughter, so Jamuna was moved to another school, but we still maintained our friendship without her mother's knowledge. I loved sitting in her house all day. Her parents were working people. She had a sister who was away at school and a younger brother who went out to rough it with the boys. For some weird reason, I don't remember eating, or even snacking, at her house. She was attracted to a guy from her new school, and she confided in me. I was happy for her, and our teen spirits were in full bloom. I gave her advice, often based on my very strong imagination. The love notes I dictated to her made the boy fall in love with her. She got nervous, and I was their companion on dates. Well, it was an obvious triangle, Jamuna was hurt, and I was friendless again.

put this sentence with discussion of mathematics I loved eating strawberry flavored peppermints while solving mathematical problems.

Life wasn't bad, but I didn't feel the loss too badly, because I met someone and fell in love as well. It lasted for five years till I turned twenty or twenty-one. I continued doing odd jobs, cleaning the house, and raising my sister's kids. Mother was working as a domestic. My other sister was busy pretending to be a high-class social worker, but she also did odd jobs as a domestic. I did the same thing for a while, but I also tried my hand at modeling and got my mug on the cover of one popular magazine. I was a runner-up in a beauty contest. I remember the judges laughing, and I thought they were laughing at me. During the question and answer, I was asked about my ambition, and I said I wanted to be a writer. They asked me what I wanted to write about, and I said the world in general and poverty. Well, I came home from the contest and decided to get my degree. I switched from science to arts and literature.

I took up sports and won a few medals for my university. Somehow, in the middle of all these activities, I managed to get my degree early, in winter. It was a Bachelor of Arts. Armed with a degree, I got my very first job in a first-rate ad agency. How did I do it? I just walked in and asked them to give me an opportunity. Yes, believe it or not, this is the truth. I was interviewed, selected, and taken in. Reading newspapers from all around the world made me feel very important. I felt I was in a different league, and the world belonged to me.

At the agency, I also got meal coupons for ten cents along with tea, snack and coffee coupons for two cents. I loved my job. I could eat almost free, I could read all I wanted, I could write. I was reborn, given a new life. Maybe during this time I shaped my life. My earlier focus on making my life different and wanting desperately to get out of misery paid off. My ambition, if ever I really had one by that name, was fulfilled. From recycling and second-hand book stores, I graduated to British Council Libraries, affordable for a $4 or $5 yearly membership fee. I could borrow books, read them, and then trade them in for still more books.

Life was beautiful, I had a job, coupons for good meals in the canteen, a whole lot of reading material, and a home with a partner. I have started believing that life is always a movie trailer, never a complete motion picture. Our life is like this so that others can script it and make a movie out of it. We who endure, live, and even enjoy ourselves can take pride in our movie.

***

Day: Amazing. What happened next?

Maya: That's all, but I have another story for tomorrow. Remember, Puggu, I have to go to work, and as I recall, you were bugging me about that. Okay, I'm off.

Day: Come on, just a few more minutes, and besides, your boss is out of town.

Maya: Hush, Puggu, never say that. Boss or no boss, I work hard. You'll have to wait for the next story. Patience is a virtue, one I have to learn, don't I? The next story is about a play I saw when I was visiting China as a journalist. You'll like it. Bye now. See you this evening.

Day: (She frowns) Okay, bye.

Chapter 3

Maya: Hi, I'm home.

Day: Ah, there you are. You're going to cook, right? You can tell your story while you chop vegetables, and I'll listen.

Maya: In China, one evening when we were sitting in a hotel lobby wondering where to have dinner, we were introduced to an actor who was also a writer. I wanted an interview right away; I needed a story, and I had no patience, But Ram Devi insisted that I watch her play first. Here's her story, as told by Ram Devi herself.

Life Is to Be Lived

Ram Devi is a woman who has lost her husband, Ramdev, and family and villagers are preparing to sacrifice her on the pyre lit for her husband. *Sati* is what they call it.

She runs away from her village in India to avoid being burnt on that pyre. She feels she has a duty to take care of her parents because she was a substitute son for them. If she lost her life, who would take care of her parents? Her sisters were too involved in the little worlds they created for themselves and were not the caring sort at all. Ram Devi flees the pyre. She is raped while trying to seek help at a nongovernmental organization, an NGO. Ram Devi, fearing humiliation and the wrath of the village, is forced to flee her village with the same NGO, but it is in reality a front for a prostitution ring in the Far East.

I am Ram Devi. I don't want to defy tradition, nor question social conditioning. All I want is to be able to live in order to take care of Ma and Baba. What am I doing in this hospital? All I remember is travelling from a village to a city and being sold to another brothel in another city. And then from one airport to another, I realize I am being taken to another country.

In one of the hotels, after a nauseating session, I felt totally lifeless, and then I found a rare moment alone. I realized I was with myself after months of torture, dulled senses and servicing pleasure seekers. To tell you the truth, at first I didn't know what I should do with the moment. I was so used to someone hovering around me all the time that I was lost for that brief fraction of a second.

If this is what freedom is, I want to use it to end my life, I thought. There was no meaning to it any more. God alone knew when I would be able to go back and take care of my parents. And even if I did get there, could I live with myself after going through so much, enduring so much? I can never face my parents; it is best that I die, I decided. I went to the washroom and splashed water on my face. Feeling calmer, I came back to find I was still alone. I prayed hard, asking God to give me some time to find something to kill myself with. I looked around desperately, and finally decided to use a bed cover to hang myself with. I tore it and tried to create a noose. I remember the noose hurting my throat, and the dreadful feeling of choking as the noose became tighter and tighter, and finally losing my senses.

Later on, Ram Devi wakes up in a hospital with a nurse beside her, watching over her as she comes to her senses. How did she land here? Ram Devi smiled a sad smile. Death had rejected her twice. Maybe life had a plan for her.

Life did have a plan for her, starting on a calm and easy day when the world was going about its normal business. She remembered how her dance with death began.

Why do I have to encounter this fate? Can I choose not to get burnt? The flame looks like a devil, and I know it is burning hot. Oh my lord, why I am thinking like a fool? They say when you see danger you lose control of your mind and I think I have lost my mind.

Ramdev was so alive when he came home last night. I know in my bones that he didn't touch a drop of daru, because I told him about how we should start planning our family. Yes, he promised, placing his hands over my womb. He had never broken a promise to me, and he said …. I don't know, I cannot think what might have happened. The sorrow of losing him has numbed my senses, but I am sure it wasn't due to daru.

Ramdev went to his older brother's home for dinner. Sukhiya is his brother's name, and Sukhmani is his wife. I could never cook like Sukhmani. Everybody praised her cooking, and people from

Chaturgaon came to dine at her place—random, distant relatives came and brought friends. Each village, of course, has one or another relative. In a way, there is always some kind of connection. In my village we do not believe in marrying our girls off to distant villages. After all, when they get old, parents need their daughters close by. This is for moral support, and besides, the bullock cart isn't good for long distance travel. I know we have three-wheelers, but they cost so much money. Most parents in our kind of villages spend their money on marrying off their daughters with a dowry.

Take my family, for instance. We are three sisters, and our only brother died when he was a child. My older sister married into a very nice, wealthy family. She has three children, and she is happy. My second sister studied till fifth standard. Then she told my mother to get her a groom, and she got married as well. I went to school too, but that was for very little time, spread over two years, something like fifty days in all, because I was the 'son' for my father. I worked in the field and helped him brew liquor. After we sold most of our land to get my sisters married off, the tiny plot we were left with wasn't enough for commercial cultivation. We grew vegetables, used most of them for our kitchen, and sold the rest in the Sunday bazaar near our village.

That money bought some groceries, seeds, and other odd items, but it wasn't enough to run the family, so we brewed liquor, mostly using molasses and rice. We had our regular clients, and the liquor money helped us to keep our home and hearth together. In this way my parents worked hard and saved money for my wedding. They got me married off to Ram Dev. All along I nursed hopes of helping my parents in their old age. I wanted to be there for them.

Now, with my husband gone, tradition demands that I go sati with him. But the flames are so hot, and I want to be a 'son' for my parents. I cannot jump into the pyre. I am committing a sin, but if I don't take care of my parents, won't that sin be greater? I am confused and scared. My mind has stopped working. But I know one thing for sure: I have to get out of this place. I need to slip away before the ladies come looking for me.

Ram Devi ventures out with her head covered with her the pallu of her saree She runs, cutting through fields and dust-covered roads. After covering a few miles, walking and running for more than five hours, she stops, because her legs give away. She is breathless, and a combination of hunger pangs and thirst pains her as well. She sees a homelike structure about 30 feet away. She gathers her strength and walks towards the house. She knocks on the door, and a lady answers. Ram Devi says, 'If only I can get a sip of water and a corner to rest my tired legs, I will be grateful to you.'

If only I had known where that knock would lead me, I would never have walked that 30 feet. Life unravels, and by the time we understand the essence of it, we are onto a different page of the book. As I write this, I unfold my saga, a bit here and a piece there.

That knock led me to hell. I did get a drink of water and food, and later on, rest. What I assumed to be fatigue as I drifted off to sleep was in fact a drink laced with a drug.

I don't know how long I've been travelling; I've lost track of time. All I gathered from hearsay and conversations with other women I managed to talk to was that the lady was a keeper for an NGO that was a front for a prostitution racket. They had a huge network that reached into different countries. Now I'm in a hospital in Beijing. Once again, death has cheated me, or I have cheated death. Maybe I've even deceived fate.

I know my peaceful moments are few. I have to plan my next step. I'm all alone and I cannot even die. I am sure I'll have to answer to the authorities, and no one will come forward to support me. I asked the nurse for water, using sign language. She gets me some water. A little later another Chinese woman with a smiling face enters and starts speaking to me in Hindi. Those words are an answered prayer. I lose myself in that moment. Her name is Ma, she tells me. It is a Chinese name, not to be mistaken for mother in Hindi. She says all this with a smile. Ma asks me what I would like to eat, and she brings me some rice and vegetables. After I finish my meal, she says that she will be coming tomorrow, and I should rest now.

Next day when I see Ma, all I want to know is, Are the authorities planning to send me to prison or send me back to my country? She just smiles at my questions and asks me to say what I would like for myself. I am not sure if this is a dream or if I'm hearing voices. How can I be allowed to speak my request? What country is this? Is this country heaven on earth? I hope it is, but I'm lost, completely. I seek Ma's help, telling her that if she could find me a job and a place to stay, and allow me to live in her country till I gather my wits, I will be thankful to her. Ma says she can try and get it organized.

A day or two later I leave the hospital, and Ma takes me with her to a tiny one-room apartment. It is small; its kitchen, living room, and dining room all rolled into one. Ma lives here and she says that I can stay here as long as I wish to. She will try to get me a job. Who is Ma? I wonder. Why is she doing all this for me?

Ma is Chinese, but she was born in India. She wanted to come back to her country of origin, but at first she was lost and didn't know what she wanted to do with her life. She worked for an international company, earning enough money to live. But she wanted more out of life, and she was willing to work hard for it. Social service was her calling, she realized, and she took it upon herself to rehabilitate the destitute. Imagine, a lady so many moons ago pushed me into this pit and here is a lady lending me a hand. Ma worked with the government, and under some secret unspoken agreement, they helped Ma with her projects.

I got work in a local library as a cleaner and volunteered for Ma in my spare time. Ma taught me to read and write Hindi and later on, Chinese. Of the languages spoken by the greatest number people in the world, Chinese is number one, Hindi is number three, and English is number two. Now I read, write, speak, and translate all three languages. I've written a play and acted in it as well, speaking the dialogue in all three languages. The audience liked it, and I was spotted by a talent company. They offered me a starring role in a movie. I became an established actor and a movie star.

Ma has advised me to write my autobiography, and publishers are ready to buy my story. To do that, I need to make a painful journey into my past. I haven't forgotten—I think of my early life every day—and now I must go back to where it started and finish what I left unfinished. I will come back to China, for this country is my home now. No matter what my parents and relatives back home might say, I won't stay there. I'll return, because I'll always be thankful to Ma and to China for rebuilding me into a new person.

***

Day: So what happened to Ram Devi? Did she come back? What did she do after her trip to meet her relatives and her publishers?

Maya: She became the famous author Ram Dasi Devi. Her books sell in translation all over the world, and one has been made into a movie. Now I need to drink some wine and relax with a cigarette. I'm just going to catch up on my reading and go to bed. Don't wake me early; I'm tired and I need my sleep. Tomorrow we'll hear about another woman who's special.

Chapter 4

Day: Maya, wake up. The milkman is ringing the doorbell. Don't you know that all that wine and no exercise will make you fat and lazy? How long has it been since you went to the gym.

Maya: For heaven's sake, be quiet. I have to answer the door and then I'll be back.

Day: Oh, coming back to bed? You are so lazy. If your health fails who will take care of you? I get so worried about you.

Maya: (angrily) How many times have I told you not to wake me up nagging at me? I know my troubles, and of course I'm scared of dying alone, or getting sick and having no one to help me. But what can I do? Didn't I try to make a home for my husband? What could I do to stop him if he wanted money, but not me? Oh, I just want everybody to go away and leave me alone, and I'm going to stop worrying whether I have any reason to or not. Besides, my story isn't as bad as the one I going to tell you. Rukmini had a far more challenging life than mine.

A Bowl Full of Life

My name is Bhargavi, I'm almost sixty years old, and I've raised two daughters and a son. My husband gambled away the family's fortunes, but he worked for the state government in Bhopal, India, and they provided us a house. Some of the neighbours were understanding and supported me in renting out rooms to make money to support us. I also ran a small catering business. I've spent my hard-earned money to educate my children, and I have managed to support my mother, Meenakshi. My mother had sold her small plot of land to help me set up funds for my family's future. I owe her food and shelter, at least.

I try to keep my mother as happy as I can. Temple is one of her favorite places, and my mother looks forward to this daily trip with me. I like accompanying her to the temple. We get to spend some quality time together. At home I'm busy with my chores, and mother is either meditating, praying, or reading. I run a household, and I have to cook, make tasty snacks at teatime, clean, and remember every member's needs. I'm trying to achieve all this on a limited budget.

This is my world. Yes, my husband is someone I'm not very proud of. Even so, I'm happy to have a husband. Still I wish at times that I had a husband who will buy me flowers and sweets and express his love. My husband does the exact opposite. When he is paid his salary, he doesn't show his face for five days to a week, depending on how much money he has won or lost.

I wish someone, anyone, from the family had warned me about his gambling addiction. My world would have been so different. I wanted to be loved, adored, and pampered. I felt so unlucky that I cursed my life and blamed fate for my misfortunes. I never got to experience a father's love. He died when I was three, and I had no brothers. I grew up with my cousins, wearing their hand-me-downs. My uncle waited impatiently for a man to ask for my hand in marriage, and he almost visibly sighed with relief when my husband's family offered the proposal. I do not complain, for I have created my little cocoon. It has given me a lot of confidence, and I no longer feel the need to blame or curse life or fate. I am proud of myself, for with a minimum of formal education, I have managed to build a future for my family.

Bhargavi has found a fabulous groom for her eldest daughter.

My daughter and her husband live in Dubai. I didn't spend much money on her dowry or their wedding, Gita and her husband Ramesh are kind enough to send me some support money every month. I am putting aside this money for my second daughter Namita's wedding. My son Nitin has just graduated in commerce, and he has a job in a multinational firm. They pay him good money.

I am planning to get him married to Seeta, the beautiful daughter of my best friend Anupriya. We used to go to school together, and we were neighbours. We shared our tiffin, worked on math problems, did our homework and exchanged moments of sorrows and happiness. Now the time has come for us to become relatives. I am happy, very happy about this arrangement. I am not forcing Nitin to marry Seeta. He likes her, and I think she has a crush on him too. Anupriya tells me that Seeta has cleared her interviews for a job in a nationalized bank. Now they can buy their own home—a corner of the world they can proudly call their own. I'm not living in a dreamland. This will happen.

Seeta and Nitin were married a year later.

I am happy and proud that I have managed my responsibilities well. All I have to do now is to ensure that Namita, my youngest daughter, makes good grades in her university and lands a good job. I am told she will make a very good architect. Let me tell you this about my children: they are all bright and intelligent, and I am proud to be their mother. Namita has already found a suitor for herself. His name is Suresh, and he works for the Indian Air Force. I like him, and I definitely approve of him. Unlike my neighbours and relatives, I do not have any reservations about love marriages. Come on, this is the 1980's. We have won the gold medal for hockey in the Olympics. Indira Gandhi has been reelected as prime minister. I may not be that well versed, but I do know that I want to make this an eventful year for my family: my mother, my husband, and Namita. I can manage this family.

My daughter has graduated. and I am inviting Suresh and his family over for dinner. My husband is happy too. Mother is sitting in her pooja room, praying for Namita's future and happy married life. Namita is looking for a job. Oh yes, the most important news of all: my husband has realized how much he has troubled me all these years. He says he had given me nothing but anxieties and worries. I accepted his apologies and made him promise he will not squander time and money gambling any more. He has taken up teaching young children. He helps them learn math, grammar, and handwriting.

Oh, my guests should be here any minute. I have made some of my south Indian snacks, including upma, kesari, parrippu vadai and coconut chutney. There will be plenty of hot filtered coffee afterwards.

They enjoyed the snacks, and we fixed a wedding date as well. In a month's time, Namita will be married. I have to make tons of preparations. This time, I have my husband by my side, and we are planning to go shopping together, since Namita is busy with her new job in a kind Parsi gentleman's firm. She will be assisting Mr Poonawala to create beautiful structures in different cities of India, and she may even work as a consultant for firms abroad.

The house is empty. The children have all gone, and I feel like taking a vacation. Maybe it would be a good idea to go and see my uncle. I was happy that he came and blessed all my children at the wedding. It is time for me to go to him and forget the unpleasantness we had. It isn't the people themselves, I guess. It's the circumstances and the stresses that make them behave oddly at times. Anyway, I have to do what's right. I plan to take my husband and my mother and pay him a visit. Maybe I'll prepare a special dish for my uncle. But tomorrow is time enough to think about these things. It's time to go to bed now. I do need to relax.

With these thoughts, Bhargavi went to bed. She woke to the sound of a dog barking and realized it was dawn. She waited for few minutes, hoping her husband would walk in with the milk can and newspaper that he always picked up on his way back from his morning walk. She got up and peeked into her mother's room where she was up and drying her saree. She was getting ready for her prayers. Bhargavi walked towards the living room and that found the front door was locked from inside. It meant her husband didn't go for his usual morning walk, and that would mean no milk for the coffee.

I wonder where he is … he lives for his newspaper. That man … she thought. Bhargavi saw a huddled figure next to the wooden couch. It was her husband. She tried moving him and found him immovable. Later that day, Bhargavi's husband was cremated. And she missed her visit with her uncle.

I can't believe my fate. Here I was, about to start living a married woman's life. I would be sharing a golden sunset and all that comes to a couple in their golden years. Never mind, maybe there's a reason why life turned this way for me. But I still have my mother, and I can play with my grandchildren as well, she thought to herself. Then she said out loud, Oh, I was so consumed by my sorrows, I forgot to tell you all that Nitin and Seeta are expecting their bundle of joy very soon. I'm getting ready to give them the best baby shower ever. Sometimes I can't handle these extreme emotions. On the one hand, I feel a deep sorrow from having lost my husband, and on the other hand, I'm happy for my son and daughter-in-law. I guess life is like that: you have to look at the brighter side and move on. I'm doing that, just as I always have.

My first grandchild is a grandson. We've all agreed to name him Amitabh. Seeta has a job, and she wants me to take care of the baby. And you know what? They want me and my mother to move in with them. I'll be moving very soon. All I need is a few days to pack and ask my neighbours to take care of my home for me. I can't sell it nor rent it, because it's part of the rent act where I was paying a minimum rent. After my husband retired, we had to give up his quarters, and we never bought our house. The company was planning to demolish the house after we left, but they knew my situation, so they decided to rent the house to us. Who knows? I might need it when I need to be by myself.

It's been a year since I moved in with my son and daughter-in-law. Amitabh is no trouble, and Mother is busy with her routine. She cooks for herself, does her own laundry, meditates. Life is more or less regularized. Nitin and Seeta go to their jobs and come back in the evenings. Some days, Nitin comes home very late, and Seeta tells me he works extra hours. Seeta is a good home manager, and she takes good care of us all. She hardly allows me to do any housework. I insist sometimes, and she tells me affectionately that I have done my share of hard work. Now it's time to take it easy and enjoy life, and I'm doing exactly that.

'Is it my imagination, or is the doorbell really ringing at this time of day? Who is it? Not a salesman, I hope.' Bhargavi opened the door to find two gentlemen asking if this home belongs to Nitin. 'Yes, it does, and may I ask who you are?' she said.

'Madam, he owes us a couple of hundred thousand.'

I was shocked. My head spun, and when it stopped, I saw that they had left and there was an envelope on the coffee table. I opened it, hoping it was a mistake and had nothing to do with my son Nitin. But it was about him. And then it hit me.

Those late night work hours that became a regular thing, and then the charming smile and change of subject when he was questioned about them. I hadn't checked the family income, but I knew the pattern, and I decided I had turned a blind eye to the same signals I saw in my husband. Nitin was heavily into gambling. I had heard somewhere that past demons have a funny way of creeping back. Did I get lost inside my imaginary cocoon, where I felt so secure? I did, and that's why I missed the signs.

When Seeta returned home after work, I showed her the envelope, and she broke down and confessed about Nitin's gambling. She was afraid I would worry, and she had a futile hope that Nitin would stop once he saw what it was doing to their lives. Poor Seeta—she didn't learn from my mistakes. Nitin didn't come home that night.

I wondered if he was out gambling away borrowed money. The couple had missed loan instalments and other payments.

I gathered my wits and mustered my strength so I could help Seeta decide what to do next. We couldn't continue to live in this big house. We considered moving back to my house, but it would only be a temporary solution. Their house had to be given up to the bank, and I asked Seeta to notify the bank about our condition. The bank gave us a fortnight's time. All this had to happen without Nitin's knowledge, of course. Nitin had called to say that he was being sent on a business trip, but we knew better. The bank refinanced the house, and the loans were repaid.

After Nitin came home, he didn't show any remorse for gambling away his family's future. He didn't even feel bad about losing the house. Once a gambler, always a gambler, I say, and Nitin was no exception. He lost his job, because the boss found out that Nitin had been flicking money from other employees. Over the years I've mastered the art of being objective, seeing my problems as puzzles to be solved, but this situation doesn't. apply. What is next in store for me? I must seek answers for myself. I must talk to Seeta and ask her to live with her parents for a time. As for me, I plan to lock the house and to visit as many religious places as possible with mother before one of us leaves for our heavenly abode.

I asked Seeta, 'What about Nitin?'

s'What about him?' she said. 'I suppose fate will decide. He will have to face his destiny. I guess and it will be about having no family and no home. This must be a lesson that God wants him to learn, because when he had all these things, he didn't value them. He blew it all. I hope that he will learn his lesson.'

Bhargavi said, 'I have to live my destiny and follow my dharma. I've done my duty towards you all. Now my mother wants me to be with her. I will see you again after she leaves for her heavenly abode. That is, if I survive.'

She left the next day, locking her house behind her. Seeta went to her parents' home and Nitin came back after his usual rounds to find the house locked and his family gone.

After almost two years, Bhargavi visited one of her neighbors. Over coffee she mentioned that her mother asked for her moksha. Bhargavi's mother walked deep into the holy river and meditated there. She found her mother's body floating on the riverbed the next morning.

What was Bhargavi all about? What would be an apt description for a woman like her? She did the right thing, no matter how difficult, every time she was challenged by betrayal and misfortune. She was courageous, she was strong, and she used all her strength and courage to take care of her family.

Chapter 5

Day: Maya, can you make an exception today and not go to work? I'm getting really interested in your narratives. I want more stories about strong women.

Maya: Okay, only because you're my confidante and I really need to hear what you think. I'll stay home, because I want to spend time with you. Work has been so hectic we haven't had a chance to talk. This next story is also about courage, but the kind of the courage is different from the first one.

A Journey of Creating Self

Sometimes courage is tested, and sometimes meeting the test is rewarded. Rukmini and her husband Subbu had three children: two daughters and one son. Their firstborn was a daughter, followed by a son and then another daughter. When their son was ten, Subbu died of a heart attack.

Rukmini was illiterate. She didn't know the alphabet, nor could she count past five or six. She was married off at an early age, and her parents never gave any importance to formal education. They wanted her to make a happy home for her husband and nurture her children, to tend to home and hearth. Rukmini didn't have any complaints, but after her husband Shiva died, her world came crumbling down. Her oldest daughter, was fourteen, her son was ten, and the youngest daughter was only seven.

Rukmini worked at a private company in Calcutta (after Shiva died, she was hired in the same company as a general help) for only a few hundred rupees. She used the money for training in typing and language skills, and she worked as a helper in a tailoring shop as well. In this way she managed to eke out a living. A year later, her oldest daughter Radha started teaching kindergarten students to recite poems and learn alphabets. While her daughter taught, Rukmini made it a point to sit with the children and learn with them. Both mother and daughter were making money to keep the family afloat.

Rukmini often tells a story about what happened to her one day that taught her she could face an emergency with courage.

Rukmini was living in a small one-room house with her children. They were at school, and Rukmini had just come home from doing some odd jobs for neighbors who paid her in either cash or in kind. Dead tired after being so busy since morning, Rukmini planned to nap for a half-hour before the children came home from school. There was a slight drizzle, and the cool air made her sleepy. She woke with a start and was shocked to find her home deluged with water. Rukmini was sleeping on a cot, and the water reached over her ankles. She had slept for over two hours, and it had rained so heavily that her house was full of water. Then it hit her that the children had not returned from school, and also that she had been cheated by the agent who helped her get this house. It was in a low-lying area that got deluged during heavy showers in monsoon season. She planned to attack that problem later. Right now, first things first.

Rukmini started out the door to search for her kids. She stopped at the doorstep and scanned people walking and crossing the road. She saw a group of school children and told herself and thought that her kids were still at school. Maybe the teachers were holding the kids till the downpour stopped. Still looking out from her doorway, she saw her children wading through the knee-high water to reach their home. She waved to them and went inside to get the bowl of rice she had saved for them the previous night. In her moment of anxiety, Rukmini didn't realize the water level had risen a couple of inches more, and that the bowl of rice had fallen off the kitchen table. In Rukmini's words, 'I saw the bowl floating and I ran to grab it. Just then I saw a dog swim through my doorway. All I wanted at that moment was to save the bowl of rice from that dog. I managed to do that, and I told myself, "I'll always meet challenges head-on."'

By means of her husband's pension money, baby-sitting, and cleaning offices, Rukmini managed to raise their living standards a little so that she could feed more than just rice to her children. She encouraged her daughter to save the money she earned tutoring kids other students. Within two years, Rukmini taught herself to read and write and got a full-time job. The three kids took care of themselves and their home, and they earned good grades in school.

The eldest daughter Radha graduated from high school and got into university, and she continued working. The son Vikram took an office job and earned some money, a useful supplement to the family income. Thus, slowly, steadily, Rukmini pulled her family from poverty to a better life with a steady income. She got her daughter married off at the right age. Her son got a good job in a leading company and earned a large salary, and he found a husband for his younger sister Neetu. Rukmini had stopped working, and her son bought a big house. She was welcomed with open arms at all three homes, those of her married daughters and her unmarried son. She spent an equal amount of time at each place and led a happy, fulfilling life with her children and grandchildren. The happy ending for this family is due to the tenacity of a woman named Rukmini.

Maya: Puggu, do you agree with what she did?

Day: Yes, but I have a question. What is the one thing that most makes a woman's life?

Maya: I'm so lost, Puggu, how can you ask me that? Okay, I'll try. I guess it's simple things. Knowing who you are, making a comfortable home. But ask me again another day, it may be something different. Let's see, what story shall I tell you? I know! But it will have to wait until tomorrow. I have to fix dinner with the radio on so I can sing with it, and then I have to wash my hair and massage my scalp to get rid of my split ends. Good night.

Day: Good night.

Chapter 6

Day: Maya! Wake up! Your pillow is covered with oil stains from last night's head massage.

Maya: I know, you can't fool me, you just want to hear today's story.

Day: That may be true. I was also listening to the news on the television.

Maya: Puggu, you have to say you *watched* news on TV. You *listen* to radio.

Day: I had my eyes closed and couldn't see the screen, so I was *listening* to the news on TV. Do you know that an aircraft with more than 200 passengers has been missing for almost 10 hours now? Oh, I have too many things demanding my attention. If you aren't ready with your story, I'm going to go listen to the news.

Maya: Don't get upset. Here's a new story for you.

If I Can't, I Will

I want to tell you about Nilima, or the iron-willed lady as I like to call her. One day, I accompanied my sister to her friend's home. To my dismay, the home was a dark room with tin suitcases stacked in one corner. I immediately stepped back out, feeling claustrophobic. While my sister remained inside to find her friend, I fell in love with a little green patch in front of Nilima's home. She grew coriander, also called cilantro, as well as fenugreek and a few herbs in a tiny garden, three feet on a side. There was a flowering tree, and beneath the tree a young man sat reading. As I eyed his thickly bound book, I heard my sister calling out my name. I ran inside that tiny cubicle and discovered tea and snacks waiting for me. Before attacking the refreshments, I asked Nilima if I could borrow the thick book from the boy sitting under the tree. I didn't care who the boy was, and I had no hesitation in asking Nilima to get it from the boy for me. In my young mind, all I knew was that I wanted that book. It turned out that the reading boy was Nilima's eldest son. She had four sons and two daughters.

Nilima is my childhood hero. To me she represents strong, solid character and endless patience. She came from a family of landowners. She had a degree from a prestigious university, and she was literate in the true sense of the word. Her husband was a strong-minded intellectual who spoke in monosyllables. He resigned his job as a math professor to open an auto repair shop in the city. Nilima moved to the city with her husband and two children. She also had twin daughters and two sons who remained in their village se left under her under a relative's care. More even than her faith in her husband's skills as an auto repairman, Nilima wanted to support her husband's hobby, and she had a backup plan. 'she will use her courage to overcome rough patches they might encounter while starting a new life in a new place' Home was a 20 ft x 30 ft room for four people to live in, including cooking and sleeping. The auto repair shop was a 4 km walk from their home.

Three years after they moved into the city, Nilima's relative sent back the two boys. She had two children of her own to take care of by that time.

Nilima's life was very restricted. Her husband demanded that she be strong, and I later realized that this meant, if the children went to bed hungry, she wasn't supposed to feel bad or get emotional about it. Rather, he said, she was to rationalize and make them understand that this was a time of struggle for them all and that it meant a better tomorrow. Most people might say that this was his personal philosophy, and why should his family bear the brunt? Each family unit follows a different philosophy, and this harsh belief is what Nilima was told to adhere to. Not only that, but she wasn't allowed to work. If she worked, her husband said, it would mean that he was weak and incapable of taking care of his family.

How exactly did Nilima run her family? To start with, her husband gave her ten rupees every day, and that represents about 35 cents. With that amount, he expected her to feed six people two meals a day. *Nothing is impossible* isn't just an adage. It was a philosophy Nilima held close to her heart. She mastered the fine art of stretching that ten rupees to feed her family two meals.

She bought wheat flour, oil, and some vegetables from the subsidized section at the green grocery. She baked exactly twelve loaves of bread or chapattis, six for the noon meal and six for dinner. On days when she needed kerosene for her stove, she sacrificed her vegetable shopping, and the family would either eat chappatis with tea or just boiled rice and its starch could fill their stomachs. Nilima's family had a roof over their heads, some food, and a business that never seemed to take off. Schooling and decent clothing seemed to elude them.

Nilima's eleven-year-old son couldn't stand the poverty in which they lived, and he left home. Nilima, waking in the night, thought

Mukund was just outside answering nature's call. After almost an hour, when she didn't hear him, she ventured out to see if he was sitting by the lamppost reading his book, but he wasn't there. In that moment, she knew he had left them. She walked back inside and told her husband, who calmly told her to go back to sleep and that he would take care of the matter in the morning. They lodged a complaint at the local police station.

Days turned into weeks, and years passed without any news of Mukund. Meanwhile, Suresh, Vijay, and Rakesh, her three other sons, got into local non-English medium schools, because education was free here. Proficiency in English is mandatory in India if you want to get a job in the mainstream. Nilima had a good command of English, so she taught them English at home, including English literature. It was a collection bought by Nilima that the oldest son, Suresh, was reading that evening beneath the tree in the yard.

That day, Nilima presented me with my very first Shakespeare collection in a pictorial format. I read Hamlet, gaping in amazement at the illustrations and trying to connect the words and the pictures. I still remember the thrill of imagining, dreaming, and creating my very own vision of Hamlet. I was just eight years old. I never got the essence of the story, but after that day, I was never lonely. My books kept me company, and I chose solitude to be with them. My love affair with books began because of that trip to Nilima's house. I read stories and dreamed of far-off places while sitting amid real life experiences at Nilima's house.

Some years later, Mukund was found in a shelter for children. Nilima's daughters came to stay with her. Suresh, Vijay, and Rakesh all received scholarships and government grants. Vijay worked hard and got his doctorate in mathematics. Rakesh got into electrical engineering and took over the business. He worked in the shop with a few assistants and then migrated to Japan. Suresh, I heard, continues to collect degrees from different universities around the globe. Nilima's daughters are university professors.

Nilima recently sent her husband back to their village to take care of their farmhouse. Free of most of her commitments, Nilima wanted to go looking for her long-lost son Mukund. After eight months of focused effort, she managed to bring her boy back home. She had a nagging fear that he would leave again, but when he did, it was to go to the university and get a degree in horticulture.

Nilima took charge of her husband's repair shop. Though technically challenged at first, Nilima worked at getting a certificate in auto parts and electronics repair. Smart lady that she was, Nilima started her careers by having professionals work for her. Later, she learned to handle minor repairs by applying all that she had learnt in her crash course. She made frequent trips to her village to take care of their farm and spend time with her husband. Her children were all settled, some married off, some still continuing their studies. Of course they were all earning and independent.

Imagine a situation where Nilima's husband didn't want her to take a job, and here she was managing a repair shop in a city and traveling to her village to keep an eye on her farm. From a traditional housewife who obeyed her husband without a whimper, to a lady living by herself and managing her husband's affairs through a long distance arrangement. Nilima has been constructive and creative tone, raised children, and held the family together. She never asserted her views and opinions, but followed the traditional marriage route and was an obedient wife to boot.

How can we describe Nilima? Should we call her a *complete woman*? Such a woman is emotionally, mentally, and physically strong. Nilima endured emotional pain when her husband made her follow his restrictive rules. Her son went missing for almost a year, and she missed meals, going hungry to serve extra mouthfuls to her children. She showed all the strengths of a complete woman.

Maya: Did you like this story? So tell me what happens with women who have a combination of all three strengths and who have to use it on themselves instead of raising and keeping a family together?

Day: I don't know. You tell me. Oh, I got it, seems like you have a tale for me. Go on I am all ears.

Maya: Not so fast my friend. I have to watch the latest Shahrukh Khan release. Today, remember, it is my date with the video player and I have ordered hot curry pizza. So, bye, bye and see you tomorrow. And yes, you are most welcome to watch the movie with me.

Day: No, I am not a cinema buff. I like words and literature.

Maya: Arre baba, movie is literature on celluloid. Anyway, it is your call. Take it easy. See you tomorrow.

Day: Goodnight Maya.

Chapter 7

It's 3:30 A.M. Maya and Day are watching a movie and having tea and biscuits.

Day: Maya, the movie is almost over. I'm not sleepy and neither are you.

Maya: Yes, Puggu, okay. What the hell, let's take a walk. There's a crisp, cool breeze outside that will clear my head. Then I'll tell you a story.

Day: Oh good, I'd love that.

If There Is a Will, Is There Really a Way?

If you have everything going for you, but your mind is filled with negative thoughts, can you imagine what happens? Akhila married when she was seventeen. Her husband, Datta, was a publisher, and they had two sons.

Today Akhila is celebrating her 50th birthday. She weighs 200 lbs and finds it difficult to move around. What happened to the lass who came to this house 30-odd years ago?

Akhila had her first child, a son named Nikhil, when she was eighteen. Datta's job kept him busy and away from home, and Akhila had time on her hands, and Nikhil sapped her energies. Akhila didn't know how to use her time effectively; in fact, she was very good at wasting it.

She was angry and frustrated, and she vented her frustration any time she could corner Datta. Their house had a huge library with authors from all over the world, but she wasn't remotely interested in reading or writing. She lived in a dream home with a huge backyard, a beautiful kitchen, but Akhila had neither an interest in cooking nor a green thumb.

Women do not necessarily have to be home managers; many are good at other things instead. Datta tried taking her with him on his tours, but she was never interested in anything but sleeping, and the reason she gave was, 'I'm homesick. I want to go back home.' Datta tried his best, but finally he came to conclusion that his wife was a mentally lazy woman, and whining was the pastime she preferred.

Datta worked hard, and Akhila had a second son. She made no attempt to change her ways. Somewhere between work, traveling, and worrying about how to deal with his wife and handle his life, Datta made way for Renuka, a young intern, to enter his life.

Renuka was an ambitious girl. She knew what Datta's life lacked, and she gave him all that and more. This was not out of unconditional love for Datta, but because she was smart enough to grab the survival ropes he offered. She cooked, cleaned, and lent him her ear and a shoulder to cry on. Datta visited her often, for she lived alone. After a while, Datta bought a house where they moved in and lived together. Akhila was happy, for she didnot haveno longer had to make any effort to cook to tend to Datta, or to listen to his stories. She called Renuka and wished her luck with Datta.

Renuka's kitchen faced west and on this day the sun was just setting. She had finished work early and was planning to cook a light dinner for herself. She rummaged through her vegetables in the fridge and found broccoli, spring onions, and tomatoes. She heated olive oil in a pan, sautéed the diced vegetables, and added garlic powder, chilli paste and salt. She rolled a few chappatis, or flat Indian breads, and started roasting. Renuka was about to roast the last chappati when her reflection appeared in the shiny metal surface of a saucepan hanging on the wall. She suddenly wondered What am I? Her thoughts continued, and she turned off the stove. Who am I? What is my identity?

She was a writer but the topics on which she wrote, were directed by Datta. He chided her often, and he never allowed her to forget that it was from him she had acquired her few social graces. He never let her forget that she was just an average writer and editor. In publishing language, he said, she lacked spark. And what is a wordsmith without a spark?

Renuka started wondering how different her life would have been if she had not met Datta. Maybe she would have known her worth herself. Maybe she would have fallen, picked herself up, and got a grip on her life. Yes, we need mentors, she thought,, but mentors who will guide us, not pave our paths. Datta sought an extension of his ego, with no thought for Renuka's individuality. And Renuka compromised herself for a few comforts and an easy route to wherever she wanted to travel. In this moment in her kitchen, she realized that a package tour with a guide wasn't her cup of tea. She would have been better off traveling and having adventures by herself.

Yes, Renuka could find a way out of Datta's shadow, but she realized it was a bit too late. No matter how hard she tried, it would be difficult for her to start all over again. She wasn't willing to give up her membership at the local club, her circle of friends that made her feel like a goddess. Deep down, Renuka knew she was basking in Datta's reflected glory, but she was enjoying it. It was only when she came home, to the house he had purchased for them, that the reality killed her spirit and made her restless. Renuka once found cooking therapeutic, but now she found it irritating when Datta asked her to cook the favorite dishes she used to create for him in the early days.

Her friends envied her when she sat next to her hotshot publisher in his car. Datta used to mockingly call himself Renuka's chauffeur. She would act coy, feeling proud to be seated next to him. Now, though, Renuka often felt like telling him she'd rather take an autorickshaw to work. Datta left her no breathing space. He was old and set in his ways, while Renuka was young and evolving.

She wanted to try her hand at a regular job and discover her real worth, but she had traded her edge for a ready-made life. She laughed, thinking about the shape she had given her life. She felt terrible every time she ran into Datta's sons. She went out of her way to please them, to stay in their good books. She couldn't mother them, for they were only a few years younger than she. All Renuka could feel, on this day in the kitchen, was a sense of guilt and emptiness. She had wasted her life cooking, cleaning, and writing meaningless words in the thrall of a man who didn't love her and who was married to someone else.

Chapter 8

Day: Maya, what do women actually want? What did Renuka want, and how different is she from Nilima, who carved her life out of stone hardship?

Maya: The difference is obvious: Renuka worked for herself and wanted to make life easy for herself. For Nilima, her own comfort wasn't very important, and that's why she enjoyed solitude and walking on the solid path she created. Look, Puggu, I can't judge other people's lives. Okay, don't laugh, I know I've done it all my life. But anyway, I'm beginning to see what men mean when they say that a woman is a mystery, a creation of God, of nature.

Day: So what's next? Who is the next beautiful creation of mother nature?

Maya: You know, since I got you involved in these tales, you're neglecting me. You don't bother to ask me how my day went. You know something? I feel ill. I don't know if I have the energy to tell you a story today. I need food. I want someone to fetch me a cup of water or maybe even a hot cup of tea. I wish I could order a take-out tea. My back hurts. I'm getting a fever.

Day: I'm laughing now. You created all this and you know it. Why did you want to live in isolation? Why didn't you share your life with anyone? You like your space so much that it's going to kill you one day.

Maya: Don't go there. I don't like anybody talking about my life. It's all very complex and with my mindset, I'm complicating things even further. I can't bring myself to trust and depend upon anyone, Puggu. When I hear tales from other women's lives, I know I can find the right path. Here's a story about trusting people. Let's see if it helps.

Day: Done. I'm all ears.

My Name Is Vidya

What is happiness? It is subjective. Some think it means having the world at your feet and everyone looking up to you. Or is it about having a significant bank balance? Or a picture perfect family? What makes a woman happy?

I know what I think will make a woman happy. If she knows her mind, if she allows her intellect to speak, even to raise its voice. I am sure such a woman will be fine. Oh, I'm sorry, I forgot to introduce myself. My name is Vidya, and that is what I told myself.

I was deluged with problems. My husband made many demands. From the beginning of every discussion, he wanted everything his way. He wanted to spend his time running his business and pursuing his interests. He didn't want to take responsibility for the kids. Most times of the time, he wanted to be away from home. I knew he wasn't the sort to have an affair, so I accepted it.

The situation was complicated, but I'll do my best to explain, After the first few years, he wanted to earn, to make a lot of money, 'just like everybody else,' he said. He sailed, we went to different countries, and after a few years he got tired of so much travel, and we settled in Australia. I did my best to manage our home and raise our children. I tried to keep my career going as well. And I wanted to know where we were heading as a family.

Because of social conditioning or for some other reason, I sought my identity through my family, so I tried to keep us together at any cost, even if it meant moving from one country to another, wherever my husband wanted to anchor his ship. I didn't want to raise my kids without a father. They must have a father at home, society says, and I was so conditioned that I followed him around the world.

In retrospect, I feel this was a waste of time and energy. If only I had told myself that I am capable, and it's better to raise kids alone than to run behind a partner who lacks parental instincts. Life would have been so different, and probably better for all of us.

My husband, like so many men, had a powerful need to be the man of the family and work tirelessly to earn money for now and for the future, above all else. Never will I get conned by that line again. It's garbage, and smart women know that!

And look who's talking sense all of a sudden. It took me 22 years of married life, until I was 46, to realize this. Women can manage everything on their own, even when it gets rough. Husbands and partners are supposed to help, not hide behind the excuse that they must make money to support the family and don't need to do anything else. That's a weak partner. He needs to be active in all aspects of raising a family with the woman.

All these years I had been managing the home by myself. I took care of sick children, handled problematic teens, made a man out of my son and a cultured lady out of our daughter. I met with teachers and principals about bad reports, low marks, even a school fight. I listened to complaints of parents saying that my children had behaved badly toward theirs. I did all this and still met my deadlines at work. When I tried to call my children's father to tell him what happened, or how lost I felt, or that I needed some help to deal with it all, he simply made the sounds of one who is preoccupied. He told me he was busy and would call me as soon as he was free, which, of course, seldom occurred. I once again would go full blast, feeling dreadful, wishing I could do a better job of handling it all. I told myself to get a grip and carry on. But I was endlessly frustrated at being stuck in this situation, and at length, I did get a grip. 'I need to stop and think,' I said to myself, and this is what I thought.

I remember that morning very clearly. My house was in a mess. I got a call from my son's school. He had got into yet another fight. I trust people easily. I take their word, not doubting intentions. I take a pretty straightforward approach to people; I take them at face value. My son had gone to school an hour early that morning. I asked him why, and he said he had an early morning presentation. How dumb could I get? Well, we all learn through our mistakes.

Later, my phone rang. I answered it, and the voice at the other end was the vice-principal of my son's school. Reliving these moments is painful, but I want to share my experiences. The man was saying that my son and two of his friends had cornered a man and hit him. And the man was bleeding. I went stiff. This wasn't the first time my son had got into trouble. In my view, he was a teenager and they often behaved badly, but I didn't know about teenage sons and how far off course they can go. I had requested a half day off work, and I had a lot of housework to do. I wanted another half-hour of sleep before I grabbed the vacuum cleaner, started the laundry, and went out to buy groceries. After I hung up the phone, it was clear that the day had other plans for me. I sat down and told myself to be calm and not to worry. I made a cup of tea and sipped it as I got dressed. Some tea remained in my huge cup when the taxi arrived. I drank it cold, put the cup in the sink, and walked out to take the 20-minute ride to the principal's office.

The incident at school wasn't earthshaking. I talked calmly with the principal, and when we got home, I had a talk with my son, making a few things clear to him. There wasn't a fight or a blowup between us, just some anger and frustration on both sides. My family was still safe, because I had handled the situation.

Then I went into my bedroom and sat down in my favorite chair to think. I asked myself, How many times has my husband bailed me out of family difficulties? Has he held my hand, calmed me down, eased my mind? How many times has he been there when I needed him?

Thinking it over, I realized what had happened. He knew I could take care of everything without having to depend on him, so he left me alone to take care of home and hearth by myself. He knew I was smart, but I didn't, so he was in control. He never acknowledged I could manage things, he just walked away, knowing I'd manage things.

I had a job, I earned money, but I thought of myself as unpaid domestic help. I never knew how much money he made. If I asked him, he didn't answer—he acted like I didn't deserve to know. In a word, he wasn't there. I did everything myself, but without getting any credit for it.

In my bedroom chair, I decided it was time to be there for myself. I said to myself, 'All these years you've been afraid you couldn't deal with life on your own, since you didn't know how you were doing. But it was the not knowing that was your greatest worry.' It was a revelation: *I don't have to be afraid to do the same things I've done all along.*

There was a time when I would have freaked out and called my husband and my friends, asking what I should do. And then all those people would have pushed their two cents' worth on me. With all this 'help' coming at me, I would have been confused and depressed for days.

Instead, on that day, I just glanced at the housework, shrugged, and got ready to go to work. I had a means of livelihood if I ever wanted to start afresh. Later that evening, during my break, I asked myself what changes I wanted to make in my life now that I had come to terms with my fear. To my surprise, I realized I didn't want to change anything.

I was okay with the my family and friends, even with my husband not being part of the family. If he wanted to be on his own, let him. I wouldn't force people to follow a familiar, traditional path. I could accept and respect their wishes. I was open to what I wanted and what others wanted. I didn't have to place limits on the family because I was afraid of what might happen if everyone would just be themselves.

Life seemed lighter and easier after that. I realized I wasn't afraid of loneliness—in fact, I loved to be left alone. Women, please try to understand. Is it loneliness that haunts you or do you not know what to do with the time that comes to you as a gift? Here's the truth: You need not 'do something' with it. It's yours. You can stare at the ceiling, or you can daydream. You don't have to make plans, or prepare for the worst, or worry about improving your coping skills. Life will go on, and things will go wrong, and you'll manage, because you always have.

The meaning of your life doesn't depend on your husband and children. If they provide vital purpose and satisfaction in your life, good for you, but life should have meaning for you even without reference to them. Having a man in your life can provide support and meaning for you not at all, a little, or a lot. Whichever it is, your life is still yours to live.

***

Maya: did you like my story? What did it tell you?

Day: I was sure Vidya would leave her husband and get a divorce. Why didn't she?

Maya: Because her situation didn't bother her any more. She found her identity, she knew her strengths. All those years, Vidya thought she needed to underplay her strengths and depend on her husband. She got a chance to make a life without him and saw that she was capable. She could respect the limits her husband set for them both without feeling compromised, that's all.

Day: So is that one of the reasons you're so isolated?

Maya: Maybe so. If one ends up living alone even after marriage or partnership, it's better to live in isolation.

Day: Well, it's your call, it's your life. What can I say? See you in the morning.

Maya: Puggu, it's very unusual for you to sign off and leave without bugging me. Okay, well, good night.

Chapter 9

Day: Get up, Maya. Did you spill wine on the carpet last night? You've been drinking again. Oh, my God, what are you doing to yourself?

Maya: Puggu, why are we women so full of bullshit about husband, children, family? We're obsessed. Why do we feel incomplete without them? I guess men feel the same, but it seems like mostly women. I need to find out how men feel about it. Okay, never mind. Here's another story. This question was brought up by a woman I met briefly on a train. She didn't tell me her name, so I let it go. We shared tea and hot samosas at a junction and that set the ball rolling. She had a passionate story to tell.

A Role Befitting a Woman

How exactly is character defined? I have talent, I have skills, I have brains. Yet I pretend I'm lost without a man.

I wonder what my role is and why I live like a corpse. Is anybody concerned about my well-being? I work hard at my job. I work around the clock to keep my home and family intact. I cook, clean, and worry. What is my worth in money? Do I have any self-esteem at all? What happened to my confidence? I used to have it when I was by myself and before I married that good-looking guy I fell for. I had it when my children were not teenagers yet. As the children grew older, they joked about my attempts to revive my hobbies and ridiculed me for being slow to grasp things.

Hey, wait a minute, I lived in a cocoon of chopping, cleaning, changing, and earning to keep things in order for the sake of family. Now when I try to understand the changed world, I am laughed at. After I got married, I was pulled, pushed, and cut down three or four sizes to conform to a set mould. I didn't mind, because I thought that was what tradition demanded. During this cutting process, I was kept in a functional mode, so that I would lend a helping hand at all times.

This functional mode was essential, you see. A level greater than this would mean, I might start thinking of helping myself. This, of course, would cause unacceptable problems and complications in a set, traditional routine.. If I got too emotional, I was suffering PMS. I was supposed to be charming and smiling all the time. 'Your charm sets the mood for everything. If you add a dash of action between sheets, there's nothing like it.' I wasn't allowed to feel too low; I wasn't supposed to feel too happy.

People told me I needed to be 'reined in'. I have heard expressions like 'I've kept you on a leash.' Wow! My guess is that I've brought all this upon myself. I entrusted myself to incapable hands, thinking they would treat me with the respect due to an individual. I didn't realize I would be treated as an object of desire, as a doormat. If I forgot to take care of my emotional, mental, or physical health, no one nurtured or encouraged me to do so. Instead, I was taken advantage of. My weak moments and vulnerabilities were exploited. Still, a little voice kept drumming in my ears: Am I a determined woman myself? Is my strength lying buried deep inside me? How and when will that strength help me to live my life, to blossom into an individual? Maybe this voice will help me to stay determined.

As a woman, I leave a piece of me in everything I do. I create a home. I raise children with lessons in character and confidence. Does all this giving of myself do any good to me at all? Does it make me stronger, or does it make me weary and weak? I create individuals and they go about building organizations. Yes, as a mother, a woman creates a man. As a wife, with her support, care and love, a woman makes a man,. Between these two roles, women give all they have, and thereby men achieve their goals.

A woman downplays her role in building up the men in her life—husband, son, father, or brother. That's a woman's courage and strength. Paradoxically, her determination lies in the fact that she is a mute spectator. After all, this man is her creation, and she doesn't want to destroy him. For that reason, some wives put up with their husbands having another woman.

Mind you, it is not that she has to put up with such nonsense. There are different women, different situations, although all such women are foolish. If he wants to look at a sleek butt, heaving bosom, or well toned body, he will go salivating like a dog behind every bitch that crosses his path. Is that all there is to being a woman? For some men, perhaps most men, that gloss and shine in a woman is good enough. As long as the gloss lasts he will stay in your kennel. It is up to you to either maintain that gloss or slash his balls and tie him to your manger.

It must be asked: Has slavery ended for us? In some cases it's physical slavery, in some cases it's mental. For some, physical slavery ends and then mental slavery begins. For some, the slavery is of all three types: emotional, physical and mental. We must be aware, and try to release other women from slavery that we might move toward freedom ourselves.

***

Day: Hmmm, that's set me thinking. I must ponder over it. I need space and time. It is deep and intense. Can I be excused now? (she smiles)

Maya: Well, if you must you must. I have a tale ready for tomorrow about a woman named Martha. I know you'll like it.

Day: Okay, let us live one tale at a time.

Maya: Goodnight, Puggu.

Chapter 10

Day: Maya? Wake up and tell me about Martha. I want to hear her story.

Maya: Okay Puggu, okay. Let me get my tea. With that and some marmalade toast I'll tell you all about her.

He Crushed Her Dreams

Numerous lanes and byways led to her house, one of those old independent houses that must have seen more than a hundred seasons. It was her ancestral property. From the outside it looked as if it needed lot of plastering and paint, but if you step inside and you must change your views. It had rare artifacts in decorative places in the ten rooms on top of the living room, dining room, library, and workroom.

Martha sat in the workroom for hours at a time to get the feeling that she wasn't old and that she had work to do after all. The days that she worked included running a farm with poultry, vegetables and a granary. She had a workforce of more than 150 men and women working for her. These were the same people whose families had worked for her grandparents and for her parents.

After she married she had to leave the house she loved more than anything else, but fate didn't forget her home. Within a year, her husband died in a car accident and Martha came back to the place where she belonged. This marked the end of her married life, and she never intended to marry again. A few years later, her parents left and she was in charge of the house. She was happy to accept her responsibilities, but she missed the guidance of experienced people like her father. She reminded herself that she was born here, and soon she would gain practical experience and run the place smoothly.

Apart from selling her farm products to nearby houses and markets, she hired people who would take her produce to far-off places as well. For this she had to increase her production, which she did in an efficient manner. People all over spoke of her ability to obtain exotic varieties of vegetables, fruits, dairy products and other essentials. This popularity, in turn, won her customers from near and far. She was able to double the annual income her father had made within two years after she took over the business. This was a time when products in other farms were produced with the help of chemicals, but nature had blessed her land with fertility. She never had to resort to chemicals and fertilizers. The news that the vegetables, fruits, and flowers were chemical-free made her a favourite with health-conscious and chemically wary people. Martha was the first choice for an overseas investor who wanted to start a fast food establishment in her town.

A man named Harry Joseph proposed that she enter into a contract stating that whatever she produced would be bought by his fast food center, for he had a vision of a healthy eatery. Her chemical-free farm suited his aim perfectly.

Martha thought about the proposal and was happy with it, except that she would be depriving her regular customers of their fresh farm products. Martha told Harry that only a part of his proposal would be acceptable to her. She said that half of product would be sold to the eatery, leaving half for the consumption of the general public. Harry was disappointed, but he agreed to her condition.

Martha took great satisfaction in striking a balance between business and loyalty. She looked around her workroom and felt happy that she had achieved so much without a companion, but a tinge of disappointment tugged at her heart, for she had no one to whom to leave her beloved farm.

Martha's thoughts wandered towards Harry, single and in his late fifties. It occurred to her that if ever he asked her out on a date, she would accept. Reaching for her mirror, she saw the face of a 50-year-old, although she was only in her forties.

Martha decided to revive whatever was left of her looks. The first step would be to take it easy on the work front. After all, her financial problems were solved. She was happy to imagine she might have a steady income after all these years of hard work. Closing her eyes, she visualized a future in which Harry proposed to her, and they might even have a baby. They would have so much to leave behind for their child, or even children.

All these dreams gave new joy to her life. Martha started whistling the tune that had been her father's favourite when he was happy. She went to her garden and drank in the scents of the orchard. Letting the aromatic air encompass her, she thought she felt a presence. Dismissing it as imagination, or just a stray breeze, she turned and saw Harry standing behind her with a revolver in his hand.

The next morning Martha was put into a coffin that was sealed with her unrealized dreams. Harry was among the mourners, and of course the police were there too. It would take them perhaps weeks, months or years to solve the mystery of the death of this lady who lived by herself. But for Harry it only took a minute to crush the dreams Martha had built with so much love and care.

***

Day: So dreaming of a better future is hopeless. Is that what you want to say?

Maya: Nothing like that. Some people find everything they want, and some people don't. In Martha's case, I'd say she was a winner even in death. She achieved a lot by herself; she was just looking forward to sharing it with someone. She wanted some sort of family, maybe just a companion in her old age. Isn't that called a golden sunset?

Chapter 11

Day: Good morning. What's next on your list?

Maya: Well, aren't you impatient? I want to leave this 'trapped in love' theme and try something more daring. Here goes.

Wild Confidence

Let us take a look at the life and achievements of a woman named Sindhu. She is a creative person who has written many books. She even won an award for her first novel. She left a broken marriage, but her spirits were intact as she picked up the shattered pieces. She simply lived her life, not seeking love, happiness and a career. She kept busy writing books, not seeking approval. She trusted her judgement and intellect. Once in fifteen years she made a passing statement about feeling lonely, but that was all.

A director made a movie out of her book, and the movie won an award. Sindhu won international acclaim with rave reviews for her creation. During her travel abroad, Sindhu met Raoul and became fond of him, but she made it clear to him that she had an agreement with a man in India. She promised to contact Raoul when she was more sure of her feelings.

Raoul was willing to wait for Sindhu's reply, and he wasn't disappointed. She said good-bye to the man in India. Sindhu, on her return to India, thought about Raoul and realized that he stimulated her mentally, she liked him, and there was emotional bonding between them in addition to their physical chemistry. She and Raoul maintained a long-distance relationship that suited her personal and professional life. She had the breathing space she needed, and she could still concentrate on her work. This went on for almost three years.

After a while, the relationship cooled. Sindhu was writing what she felt was her masterpiece, and Raoul tried his best to keep their romance alive. Then Sindhu met a man who wanted her to be by his side. His name was Harish, and he wanted Sindhu to move with him in his huge ancestral home. He even was willing to let her call the shots.

Things went well for Sindhu, and an American movie production company offered her a job as a scriptwriter. She flew to California on a three-week contract and found Raoul there to lend her moral support. The moment she saw Raoul, she realized she still had feelings for him. Soon she saw that she was in love with him. What about Harish? her mind screamed. Sindhu had found love, but she loved two men equally. She completed her contract and returned to India.

Harish threw a lavish welcome home party, inviting people from the A list of celebrities, from a German actress to a UN ambassador. The ambience was from every country: Thai food and sake, French cuisine and champagne, couture gowns and international gossip glittered in Harish's ballroom, all to welcome her. Sindhu thought for a moment of Raoul, but then she saw Harish, danced with him, and luxuriated in the magnificent life he offered her.

A week later, Sindhu discovered she was pregnant. She was delighted, and she called her friend Gita not only to share her news but also to drop a bomb on her. 'Yes, I know, isn't it wonderful! But I tell you what, I need a DNA test. I have no clue whose baby this is. I was active with Raoul in California, if you must know, and then after that great party, Harish wanted to seal the relationship. You know, these things happen. No, I didn't use birth control—for heaven's sake, don't yell at me, Gita! Just tell me where I have to go to take the test.'

That was Sindhu, of course: bold, open, independent, not to be pinned down. Harish didn't know how to handle the news—he simply stood there, struck silent. Raoul asked her to marry him, saying that he wanted to support her. Gita asked Sindhu bluntly, 'Okay, girl, what are you going to do now?'

'Gita, one thing is sure: I'm not going to get a DNA test. I want the child for myself. It doesn't matter who the father is. I don't want to know. This is *my* child.'

Those nine months weighed heavily on Sindhu. Gossips sneered at her, friends and family kept their distance. But through it all she kept her head high. She had twins and named them Divit and Dishant. The moment her family saw the babies, they folded all three of them into their arms.

Sindhu would have survived and thrived in any case. She always did what she wanted to; she carved a niche for herself with her writing and etched her identity in the community in which she lived. As an unwed mother, a creator, a woman who made her own rules, is she happy? Isn't woman by nature one who creates? Sindhu is that in every way, and she's happy.

***

Day: How did Sindhu's family react? How did her friends take it? Was it difficult for her?

Maya: Puggu, a woman knows best, let's leave it at that. She senses things and somehow knows how situations will work best for her.

Chapter 12

Maya: Puggu, Puggu, wake up. I hear something—some kind of sounds over at Radhavi and Shiv's house. I hope Shiv uncle is okay.

Day: That guy is crazy. He must be hitting the old lady. You know she's lazy and he's wired.

Maya: Shut up, Puggu. Show some respect. They're our neighbours. Let me go and take a look. It really seems like something's wrong.

Silent Courage

When Maya enters Shiv and Radhavi's bungalow, she finds them packing their belongings. She wonders what has happened to make them take a vacation, or even leave permanently. The look on Shiv's face is not that of a person who is about to take a vacation. Instead he looks concerned, even frightened.

Maya: Uncle, what's happening? Is everyone okay? Radhavi, why are you packing?

Shiv: It's fine, Maya, everything's okay. We just want to stay with our sons and take care of our grandchildren.

Maya: Why the sudden decision? You were going to rent space to me for my work as a designer.

Shiv: Yes, I remember. Please accept my apologies—I'm sorry I have to leave without keeping my promise to you. My son will be here in a week or so to put the house up for sale.

Radhavi enters and smiles a weak smile at Maya. 'Hello, Maya. Come and have coffee with us. I know you like my coffee. Here, sit down.'

Maya: Auntie, why such a sudden decision? What will happen to Nivedita at the university? She dreamed of making it big in Bollywood.

Shiv: Oh we're sure she will do just as well in Hollywood.

Shiv tried to laugh, but the sound she made wasn't a laugh at all.

Maya knew something was really wrong. Shiv and Radhavi were not the sort of people to make impulsive decisions. I saw them just last week. What could have happened in such a short time?

She wanted to ask them, but how could she without being nosy and rude? After a few minutes' thought, though, she realized she must find out.

Maya: Please, Uncle, I'm concerned for you. Please tell me what has gone wrong for you. I won't speak of it to anyone. Trust me, for I care about you both and I will not betray your confidence.

Radhavi and Shiv exchanged glances and sighed, for they knew that Maya would ask this. 'Make yourself comfortable,' Radhavi said. 'The story is a long one.' Radhavi poured more coffee for everyone and began to tell Maya what had happened.

On the way back from the university late one evening, Nivedita felt she was being followed. She paid little attention, but she should have been wary, because an unusual thing had happened not long before. A boy she knew was bringing her home on his Vespa. As she stepped off the scooter, a figure emerged from the shadows. He told her that she was being watched and that 'they' didn't like her activities. Nivedita was taken aback. She was being watched? She hadn't a clue why, or who 'they' might be. She decided they had mistaken for someone else. Nivedita gave no thought to the incident and went about her routine. Sometimes she rode home with her friend, sometimes she walked home alone.

A few days later Shiv found a note in an unaddressed envelope with his name scribbled on it, lying on the verandah.

Shiv took up the story from where Radhavi left off.

After my nap, you know, I go out to the porch to pick up the evening newspaper. I still want to read my news, not watch it on TV. I looked down and saw an envelope with my name on it in handwriting. I brought it inside and called Radhavi, and we opened it together. The note inside had an X mark in red, showing a stop sign or a traffic light or something. I didn't know what it meant. There was no signature. Strange things had been happening for several days before: the phone would ring and when we answered it, there was no response on the other end. One evening Nivedita was later than usual. I felt restless, waiting. It was unlike her, for she was very conscientious. She is very aware that we are her guardians, her parents are working hard in the U.S. for her sake, and we take very seriously our responsibility for her. She arrived a full three hours late—it was almost midnight. When she got home, we were furious. Why did she not call us and say she'd be late for dinner? And why had she had been out until midnight? But she looked upset, so we all sat down to talk. Nivedita apologized and told us what had happened.

She had finished her lectures and was walking towards the bus stop. On her way, she felt like having a coffee, so she stopped at a café and ran into some classmates. They spent almost an hour at the café, talking about their plans for next year, what they would do during the holidays, all the usual things students talk about. They lost track of time, and Nivedita realized she had missed the last bus. A friend offered to drive her home. As soon as the car stopped in our driveway, a figure emerged just as before. Two men forced Nivedita back into the car, got in after her, and gave her friend directions to an unknown destination. After driving for about 25 minutes, Nivedita and her friend were taken into a bungalow. By now both kids were scared. They didn't know what was happening to them. They went into the house without resisting and were told to sit down on a couch.

A little while later a bearded man wearing a kurta and a loose jhubba entered and smilingly offered them drinks. After putting a tray of drinks on the coffee table, the man took hold of Nivedita's hands and told her she was being watched, just as the other man had said. It seems that their group didn't approve of the dresses she wore, or that different males escorted her home. As you know, Nivedita wears clothes like any other modern girl would wear. She treats people with respect, she isn't biased about gender, and she isn't a prude.

Nivedita didn't know what to say. As far as she was concerned, her dresses were perfectly okay. A shoulder shown here, a skirt just touching her knees, slacks, tight and trendy jeans maybe. And she had male friends who had cars and motor scooters. What's wrong with all that?

As she told her story, it hit all three of us at the same time. We were being attacked by so-called moral policing. I know what you're thinking: Why is this 'moral policing' enough to make us decide to leave here? Maya, you probably don't know about this. Don't be shocked, for it is the truth.

Apparently a male student, a nonhindu, has been missing for almost a week now. Nivedita heard that the boy's parents were asked to identify a body in a general hospital. It was indeed their son. There was a head injury. He may have been hit with an iron rod or something similar. Now do you see why we have to leave? Those who kidnapped Nivedita are using violence to enforce their strict views.

Maya: Auntie, say something, please. Is there no other way? Do you have to leave? Uncle, if we leave town because of fear, who will remain and stand up to these people? In the name of moral policing they're making rules and terrorizing those who don't follow them. This is outrageous, it is bullying.

She didn't get an answer from her aunt and uncle. Maya left the bungalow, feeling cold and shaking her head in disbelief.

***

Day: Maya, I know you tried your best. Don't be too harsh with yourself.

Maya: But Puggu, I know auntie has it in her. She can fight it with Nivedita's help, but uncle will not permit them to stand up against the bullies. He is the head of the family, so he's making the decision.

Day: Maya, hurry up, I hear their vehicle outside.

Maya: Puggu, it's too depressing. I don't want to watch them leave.

Day: Maya, don't forget your manners. You have to say good-bye to your neighbours; It's their last day. Go out now, and greet them and wish them well.

Maya returned, looking happier than Day expected.

Maya: Puggu, you aren't going to believe this. Radhavi told Shiv to go on to Atlanta with Nivedita. She's staying behind for a while and will follow them to America later.

A few weeks later, Maya had news of Radhavi.

Maya: Puggu, I have to tell you, Radhavi lodged a complaint against those people. She didn't have their names, so she met with some neighbors who had faced similar problems. They were hesitant, but they agreed to support the cause. The women went to see the local Member of Parliament, the Inspector General, and the Legislative Assembly. They told their story to all these people simultaneously so that if the local police didn't take action when they complained, either the MP, the IG or someone else would investigate and punish these hoodlums. Radhavi received an award from the mayor at a function specially organized for her and the women who stood up with her. It turns out that aunty has a double MA—postgraduate degrees in social sciences and world religion. I would not have guessed that she could be so powerful. So, Puggu, do you think I did the right thing by interfering in their affairs?

Day: I'd say you did just the right thing.

Chapter 13

Maya: Puggu, I have a story for you from Canada. I was having tea with Revathy and the daughter of a friend of hers married a guy living in Canada.

Day: Canada, brrr, all I know about that country is that it's cold even in the spring. Tell me about your friend's daughter. What happened to her?

Maya: You've made me feel cold, I'm going to get under the covers. Okay, here goes.

Some Warmth and a New Life

Uma felt light and happy. A fresh breeze flowed through her hair, her arms were beautiful, covered with henna. She had married and now she was in Canada. She had been here only a week and she was already in love with the country.

Today she had applied for her health card. Sitting with her mother-in-law, sister-in-law and husband Veer, she felt secure and comfortable. Her sister-in-law, Shika, Uma felt, was a simple girl in jeans. She had expected Shika to be very modern. Her husband's family had lived in Canada for twenty years, so Shika was able to be modern, western and Canadian. Uma fell in love with everyone in the family; she felt they were not at all Canadians. They were just uncle and aunty from her neighborhood in Chandigarh. The only person missing from the family portrait was 'uncle' father-in-law who had died a few years ago. Otherwise, this is a perfect family picture, thought Uma.

After a few days, Asha, her mother-in-law, briefed Uma on the routines of cooking and cleaning. Asha had to leave for work, and of course Veer had a job. Shika went to the university and worked part-time in a store.

Uma had a new life, a new country, and she loved it. When she got up in the morning, she planned her day, packed lunches for everyone, and then did the cooking and household work that was required. Each person had a different schedule, and she enjoyed this, because it kept her busy. After a few months of being a good housekeeper, though, Uma felt that Asha and the others weren't as happy with her as they had seemed at first. Uma tried not to let it bother her too much, but the housework had increased. She tired easily and began to feel useless. She was homesick and wanted to see her parents. This was the beginning of the nightmare that her life became.

When Uma said she missed her parents, Asha asked her where she thought the money for her travel would come from. Uma had no idea, all she knew was she had been here doing the cooking and housework for all these people for four months, and she could see nothing wrong with taking a few weeks to visit her parents. After all, her family had spent many rupees, including the dowry, the marriage expenses, and other things.

Asha had told her parents that they owned a big business in Canada, so Uma felt a bit odd when Veer, Asha, and some days including Shika, all went to work in the morning. She asked no questions, being a simple girl from a small village. She thought this was normal for people in Canada. She was impressed when she saw that Shika dressed in a very simple style. Now she wanted to ask what had happened to all that money and why could she not have some of it to buy a ticket for her to India?

Just a straightforward question to Asha about why she could not travel was all it took for Veer to give her a resounding slap across her cheek. Uma was stunned and didn't know how to react. Her world came crashing down. Uma had heard stories about how girls were abused, and it looked as if her name had been added to the list. She thought about what was happening to her, and she decided not to take it lying down.

Uma had never ventured far from the house except to take a walk or shop for groceries. It was still summer, and she had yet to get her driver's licence. What should she do? She didn't sit down and worry about what would happen to her. Instead, she walked to the grocery store and told her story, and the kind owner helped her by calling the police. They put her in a shelter.

At the shelter, she had a home all right, but her documents were with the family and it would be a while before she got them. Mustering all her courage, Uma started asking for help and learning how to go about living life in Canada. She was put in touch with agencies and community centres. She took vocational and language classes, and after a few weeks at the shelter she landed her first job as a cashier in a local supermarket.

That job gave her her first money, and money is a powerful tool if you know how to use it. Uma decided to go back to school. She saved money for school, and three years later, Uma graduated in Media and Communications and landed a job as an intern at a television station. In a few months she was hired by the rival station for a hefty salary. Was she good at her job? According to the local media circle, she was an outstanding reporter. Her coverage was so good that the station decided to start a segment for Uma. She covered women's issues and created an awareness campaign through her reporting. After a few years in the public eye, she wrote two books and started a chain of stores, including a flower shop, a coffee shop. and a bookstore.

Chapter 14

The day has not begun very well. Maya is sick and Day is sick with worry for her.

Day: Maya? Are you okay? It's all right, I'll take care of you. Please take a sip of water. You know I always worry about your asthma. I'm calling the doctor. Just lie still, you're going to be fine, you're strong. I'll have no meaning to my life if you don't spice up my days. I wish you'd take better care of yourself—you drink, you smoke, you stay up late at night. Oh, Maya, I'm sorry. Forget I mentioned it. Anyway, I'm going to tell you a story while you get your strength back. Do you remember that weak woman named Sasha who had three daughters?

Spice in Their Lives

Sasha was forty-eight, and she knew she had only a few years to live. Ram had left her for another woman. Sasha gazed up at the sky and dreamed as she squeezed the dishwashing liquid over the plates and bowls. Tomorrow will be another difficult day for Sasha. She'll go to work at the restaurant and come home dead tired. Her bones are getting weaker and weaker, and she feels heavy with weariness and frequent bouts of fatigue.

Sasha didn't want to burden her daughters; all three, Vidya, Pria, and Mira, were very young. Sasha earned enough to feed and clothe them and to keep a roof over their heads. Saving money for the future wasn't possible.

Sasha celebrated just one festival: she made it a rule to celebrate Ganesh Chaturthi. 'He is the *vignahartha*, (the one who will guide in conquering all troubles) and I'm sure he will find a path that will lead me towards peace.' In the next couple of days, she knew, the lord of good luck would be coming home. Today was her day to shop for rice flour, jaggery, and cardamom to make the modak, a sweet treat for her lord.

After rinsing the dishes, she made a grocery list and informed her daughters that she was going to the grocery store. She bought fresh coconut, flowers, fruits, and other things and walked home carrying her bag. On the way, her eyes fell upon a movie poster. It was an old Amitabh Bachchan and Rekha movie. She remembered the days when she went to movies, dined in restaurants, and read books to her heart's content.

She thought to herself as she trudged homeward, It's been years since I watched a movie in a theatre. Why is life so tough? Why can't I have a normal life, the kind where couples go to movies, eat out, take vacations with their children, and do the things that families do? Why do I have to suffer and feel no peace? Will I never have any more than this? Must I accept my lot without complaint?

By this time she was halfway home, and she shifted the grocery bag to her other hand. She imagined what life would be like if she didn't have to carry this bag and keep putting one foot in front of the other. Perhaps she'd be preparing dinner while Ram and the kids were getting ready to surprise her with tickets to a movie and reservations for dinner.

Life gives us much that we aren't ready for. Actually, we're never ready for all that life gives us; we just get used to it after a while—except for falling in love, and its hopes and expectations. Sasha knew about those expectations, and the way the magic vanishes. She wasn't ready for death, even if life wanted to give it to her. Sasha wanted to settle her daughters, and she needed a better job. Life didn't want to give her that. She was qualified for jobs that were sophisticated and required intelligence, but with three daughters to take care of, all she could do was raise them. If she chose career and self-development over raising her children, there would be an imbalance of a kind she couldn't imagine. She dare not take the chance.

Why was she chosen to take all the suffering and why was Ram getting off scot free? To add to her woes, she had been diagnosed with cancer. Sasha put her groceries on the kitchen table and made a masala tea. The aroma of cardamom and ginger calmed her nerves as she brewed her tea. She loved this part of her day. Sasha looked in the mirror and smiled to herself. She had read somewhere that if you smile at your reflection repeatedly, it will make you into a positive person. She needed all the positive energy she could gather. But no matter what, the same thought came back: What will my daughters do if I leave them for my heavenly abode?

The next evening, Sasha again travelled the path of thought, picking up the trail from the day before. Chopping vegetables and thinking, she looked at the bulky seed cluster in the eggplant. She called out to her daughters 'Vidya, Pria, Mira, come down and look here, in the kitchen.' Vidya looked at the strange expression on her mother's face and said, 'Okay, Mom, tell us what you have.'

Sasha was still looking fixedly at the eggplant center. She handed the center to Pria and said, 'Your job is to see that this pulp is sundried and brought back to me after a week.'

A week later Pria and her sisters brought the sundried eggplant center to their mother. Sasha carefully laid a piece of muslin on the table, placed the eggplant on it, and collected the seeds. She distributed them among her daughters.

'This is life,' she said, 'and I'm sure you'll learn its lessons. I want each of you to make your life using these seeds.' The daughters were well behaved and honored their mother, so they didn't question Sasha's request. Each one did what she thought was the right thing to do.

Vidya bought soil and sowed the seeds. Pria and Mira did the same. Seeds germinated and tiny green shoots started peering out of the soil. Pria, Vidya, and Mira tended their plants attentively. After a while, Vidya and Pria's sections of the center started bearing fruit. The young eggplants were a rich green, and as they ripened they shone with a deep purple hue. Vidya picked some and made three different dishes: Eggplant Sambar, eggplant with spices, and Baigan Bhartha.

Eggplant Sambar

2 medium eggplants
1 cup toor dal
1 tablespoon coriander seeds
1 cup coconut
3 long red dry red chillies
1 tablespoon chana dal
1 teaspoon mustard seeds

1 teaspoon fenugreek seeds
3 tablespoons oil
A small lemon size ball of tamarind
1 small sized onion
1 small sized tomato
Pinch of asafetida and turmeric.

Pressure cook the dal. In a pan heat the oil and add mustard seeds and fenugreek seeds. Add the chopped vegetables and fry them for a minute. Add the tamarind water, turmeric and asafetida and salt to taste. Grind the coconut and red chillies to a fine paste and add it to the boiling tamarind mixture. After about five minutes add the dal. Allow it to boil and cook it on low fire for few minutes. Serve with white steamed rice.

Eggplant with spices

6–8 eggplants of the small variety	2 tsp sesame seeds, roasted separately to a light brown
oil for deep frying	
1/4 cup oil	2 tsp tamarind paste or to taste
1/2 cup onion, finely chopped	2 tsp salt or to taste
1/2 tsp each garlic paste, ginger paste	1/4 tsp turmeric
1/4 cup grated dry coconut	1/2 tsp powdered red pepper
1 tbsp coriander seeds, roasted light brown	7–8 curry leaves
2 tsp cumin	1 tbsp coriander for garnish

Slit the baingans (eggplants) and deep fry over high heat till glossy and a little tender. Remove from oil and set aside. Grind the coconut and the roasted coriander, cumin, and sesame seeds together, using a little water if need be. Heat the 1/4 cup oil and saute the onions, ginger and garlic till onions are soft and a little transparent. Add curry leaves and turn around, then the ground mixture, and sauté till the oil separates. Add the tamarind paste, salt, turmeric, and red pepper and mix well. Then add the baingans. Turn around a few times. Add about a quarter cup water, bring to a boil and simmer, covered, for about 5 minutes. Serve hot, garnished with the coriander.

Baigan Bhartha

2 large (750 gm) eggplants (baingans)
2 cups onions, chopped coarsely
2 cups tomatoes, chopped coarsely
1 tbsp ginger, finely chopped
1 tbsp ginger, finely chopped
3–4 green chillies, slightly slit
1 tsp cumin seeds
1 tbsp powdered coriander seeds
1/2 tsp garam masala
1/2 tsp turmeric powder
1/2 tsp powdered red pepper
2 tsp salt
1/4 cup oil
1 tbsp chopped coriander leaves for sgarnish

Roast baingans over a medium flame till it gets a charred look, and sometimes the skin splits also. Place in a container of water, and when cool peel off the charred skin and cut off the stalk. Chop fine. In a heavy-based saucepan, heat the oil and add the cumin seeds and when these splutter add the onions and the ginger and sauté over high heat, till the onions get a slightly fried look. Add the tomatoes and the green chillies and continue sautéing till the whole mixture looks glossy. Add the coriander powder, garam masala, turmeric, salt and red pepper and stir a few times to mix well. Add the eggplant, stir a few times over high heat and then lower the heat and cook till done. Serve hot, garnished with the coriander leaves.

Vidya sent free samples to her neighbours, and in a week's time she had three families asking her for homemade meals. Pria gathered eggplants from her section and sold them from a temporary stall across from their house. She decided to invest in fertilizer, garden tools and bags to pack her produce. Since Mira was more of a dreamer and liked to lend support, she concentrated on helping Vidya and Pria.

And Sasha? She was a proud mother who taught her daughters the art of living life using eggplant seeds. The family of four managed to set up a small catering business using fresh produce from their farm. They used natural fertilizers to grow vegetables and fruits, and they called it organic produce. Caterers and vegetable suppliers were eager to buy from them.

Mira was the dreamer—she wanted to grow and reach out. Vidya made Mira see sense and explained how important it was for them to build a strong foundation and sustain what they have before moving to the next level. Their business grew steadily. and their lives grew as well.

Sasha was cured, and she found peace in watching her girls live their lives. Vidya and Mira got married. Pria opted out of marriage and got into entrepreneurship. She went abroad and got a degree in business management. After that she took a crash course in farming, and she came back and made a name for herself. She adopted two children.

Sasha tries to spend equal time with all her daughters. Inspired by then, she volunteers at a local Red Cross Society and organizes food festivals and flower shows.

***

Day: Maya, are you feeling better?

Maya: It was inspiring. I like Sasha's subtle motivation—I admire her a lot. You already know that, so what's next? Another powerful tale of a mother, a wife, a sister?

Day: Oh, no. It's your turn now. I'm tired taking care of you and your asthma attack.

Maya: Fine. My story tomorrow will be about a woman who learns about herself and her ambition. You let me know what you think of her. She's someone I've met, someone I know.

Chapter 15

Day: Maya, are you planning to take it easy and narrate your story today?

Maya: Puggu, I'm off to the doctor first. Then I want to go grocery shopping.

Day: Why do you need groceries?

Maya: I have to take care of my health. I want to lose weight. I want to stop ordering take-outs. I want to eat salads and soups.

Day: Hahaha, don't make me laugh, Maya. No take-outs? Salads and soups? That's rich. One thing that's consistent about you is your inconsistency.

Maya: Stop it or I won't tell my story today.

Day: Okay, Maya, I'm sorry. Let's see, you said it was about an ambitious woman, right?

Maya: Come sit in the kitchen with me and I'll tell you the story while I make a salad.

Hello Ambition

The stage was all set for her performance and she was waiting in the wings, ready to enter on cue. The auditorium was packed to capacity, and people were waiting outside trying to gatecrash just to take a look at their favorite singer. Riyala was still reigning over the entertainment industry after many years. She had been a singer since she uttered her first words: *do, re, mi!*

Riyala's mother, Stephanie was a single parent who raised her to become a professional singer. Stephanie knew from the time her daughter was a baby that her voice could be trained into greatness. Stephanie made sure Riyala got the instruction she needed. She started strong as a child prodigy, and her performances were extraordinary. She had several patrons to support her.

Riyala hardly had any time to be a child, and she stepped into adulthood wanting nothing more than to perform, tour the world, and promote her songs. She hoped her music would reach every corner of the globe. She understood the industry, and how to generate the contacts and timing that would realize her dream. Love and relationships didn't enter her into her plans; all she wanted to do was perform, and she would go any length to achieve her goals. It was all she thought about.

Riyala was passionately devoted to her craft. If she wasn't performing, she was rehearsing or talking to knowledgeable people about music, for she was known for the authentic and original sounds she produced. She toured Egypt, Kuwait, Dubai, Africa, Montreal, Austria, and more. She spent more time in nature, walking on byways and in forests, than in the comfort of luxurious hotels. Riyala's many fans loved her and respected her authenticity.

Riyala knew that her fans always wanted more new and original music from her. Sometimes she felt that they were like children demanding more and more from her, Riyala, and only her. Even in the face of this demand, Riyala wanted to respond to their needs and not disappoint them. She became so deeply involved in her music that she hardly knew where she left off and her music began. At 24, she had few personal relationships, and men who wanted to be close to her realized that it was her music and her audience to which she was devoted, not to them. She wanted her time with them to be for pleasure, not for commitment.

Once, a teenager with whom she had spent time in intimacy was unable to get her out of his system. He was studying for a degree in international media studies and met Riyala as part of his course project. The interview session led to sipping coffee in a corner café and then to a freewheeling chat session that went on till the wee hours of the morning. After a while, it was clear that he worshipped her.

Teenage years are emotional ones, and it's easy to get carried away. The object of such extreme feelings needs sensitivity and maturity to be good to the young person and still see that they both step away from an unbalanced relationship. Riyala, who didn't have such sensitivity and maturity, did what she had always done: she had fun for a while and then became indifferent to the boy. But he wanted a commitment, even after such a brief courtship. Getting no response from her caused him to become crazed and then obsessive. He phoned her, stalked her, and even wrote letters to her in his own blood.

Riyala couldn't shake him. She tried explaining to the lovelorn boy that it wasn't possible for her to make a commitment. No matter what she did—sweet words, tender but firm discussions, angry outbursts—she couldn't persuade him to leave her in peace.

Finally she thought of a plan that might work. Riyala dialled a number, and the voice at the other end answered in monosyllables.

She spoke for a few minutes, hung up the phone, and poured herself a drink. At last she was free of the stress she had endured. She wanted to erase the memory of those recent weeks and give her full attention to her performance.

It was opening night, and Riyala was backstage preparing for her entrance when a woman whispered something into her ear. Riyala nodded and looked up as if thanking someone for a divine intervention, but she knew better. Riyala had plotted to kill the young man with the help of a waiter from the same corner café where they had met.

She raised her head, ready to go onstage, the place where she wanted to be, where she was fully herself. She paused briefly, though, and remembered the beautiful moments she had spent with this boy. Funny, she thought as she made her grand entrance, "I never even knew his name."

Chapter 16

Maya: Puggu, I've got a story about a woman named Mallika who's different, who has so many aspects. She always leaves one situation and goes to another, looking for something perfect rather than creating something good for herself. While she looks, she learns the balance between the situation and her part in it.

Part 1
Experimenting with Boredom

My friend Mallika was a confused creative sort of woman. She was a dancer who had won dance competitions. She flirted with writing, but she wasn't an author. She wrote random stories and articles for journals. She was a cross between an author and a journalist, with a little of the dancer in her. She said her real interest was to get married, but marriage wasn't really what she wanted either.

She knew she lacked the edge to pursue writing as a career. She liked spending time with her friends, but she didn't really miss them when they weren't around. Mallika was confused and also confusing to others. In the end, she decided to get married because she couldn't think of anything else to do at that point in her life. Soon after her marriage to Anand, she moved away and had twins, but marriage and two children wasn't enough for her. She wanted both her old lifestyle and her new one.

In the old days, Mallika sipped tea and whined about how boring life was without hubby and baby, but now she thought it was even more boring with hubby and babies. She reached a point where she thought her life had no meaning. She had reached a sort of midpoint, unable to find herself in either way of life, past or present.

This was when she knew she had to find her way out of that point of being nowhere. Instead of calling her friends for a whining session, she straightened her shoulders and looked in the mirror.

Who was she? Was she what her friends saw in her? Was she a wife and mother who dressed up and celebrated festivals? Was she a journalist, an intellectual, a thinker? She knew she had to peel away the layers and reveal her true self to herself first. She had to be honest and feel her true feelings instead of just wishing for something else.

Mallika was small town girl who had aspirations of living in a high-rise penthouse dreaming, writing, creating. But she also wanted to be the ideal wife, mother, and friend, so she let go of her calling and played a game of pleasing everyone. All the while she misled herself and others by pretending she wasn't just pleasing her near and dear ones, but also living her own life. All the time, she knew this wasn't true. She had spun a web of self-deceit for over thirty years. Could she break free from its entanglements? What should she do? Live in her safe cocoon? Until she decides to break free, she will live a lie. Mallika is suffering from the contemporary woman's problem: she's a cross between a modern woman and a traditional one.

After a heart-to-heart chat with herself, she decided marriage and kids were not her life, but someone else's life she was living. One Sunday morning when Anand and the twins were fast asleep and the morning papers and milk were yet to be delivered, Mallika left a note on the kitchen table.

Dear Anand,

I tried my best to take care of this marriage, and you and the kids, but it looks like I'm not prepared for this. I need some time away. I'm so sorry, but I need to seek myself and attend to who I really am. Take care of the kids and please ask our friends and family to forgive me.

Goodbye,
Mallika

Part 2
Experiments Continue

With some money and jewellery, she took a train to a local hill station and booked a room in a cheap youth hostel. She paid 500

Rs for ten days and another 100 Rs for simple vegetarian food. She bought some wine and couple of books. On the second day, she met Subhash, a dancer. Mallika felt perhaps this was her destiny calling her. Maybe this was her chance to create a troupe of dancers and tour the world.

There were dreams and dreams, but reality was this: she would wake up at four in the morning and start cooking lunch. She would tidy up, wash clothes, and get ready to leave by 7 a.m. to catch a train so she could be at work by 9 a.m.. If she missed that train, she had to change trains twice, and she dreaded that. Mallika told herself, This is just a temporary situation. Subhash will get a better job and my problems will be solved. He had mentioned a ballet that a big dance company was planning and said he would be one of the dancers, but that didn't happen.

A few months after they moved in together, Subhash said he wanted a child. Mallika wasn't ready to make such a commitment, and that day was the first time he hit her. After a while she became accustomed to being abused both verbally and physically.

She was forced to spend the money she earned buying liquor for Subhash in addition to providing for both of them. He was getting frustrated facing rejection after rejection. He even started cursing Mallika for bring him ill luck. He had a few dance students, but they stopped coming to him. She began to feel cursed herself.

Mallika slogged through her days feeling like a slave. She was trapped in a vicious cycle of emotional blackmail. Subhash used all the clichés: How will I live without you? Who will take care of me? He even said he loved her, which was shown to be a lie every day. By now she realized that just having rhythm doesn't make one a professional dancer, and that having a troupe and traveling the world comes only with talent, passion, and dedication to the art.

She was facing the same problem as she had with Anand. Mallika definitely didn't want to stick it out with this drunkard She didn't love him, so why was she with him? She wasn't sure, but she knew how she'd leave him. It sure wasn't with a note and an apology. She would pretend to go to work and she wouldn't come back.

That morning as she sipped her tea, she knew where she'd be heading. As she left her tiny dwelling, she heaved a sigh of relief. She took a train, and fifteen minutes later she was at the airport buying a ticket to Aurangabad.

Part 3
Concluding Her Experiments

Sitting in her green room, Mallika stared at her reflection in the mirror. Thanks to the rigorous routine of disciplined practice, she had mastered the dance form she loved. Her guru was proud of her, and he had chosen her to perform at the Presidential Palace. Mallika was thrilled and wanted to share this news with her family. She now had a second husband, a daughter, a loving mother-in-law and a challenged brother-in-law. Mallika found out that her family would be here in two days. She could phone them, but she wanted the joy of sharing the good news in person.

Mallika knew she had been very fortunate to meet Sukesh in Aurangabad. When her plane landed that day, she booked herself into a small hotel, and next morning she visited a popular temple. At the temple she saw family struggling to push a gentleman in a wheelchair, and she ran to give them a helping hand. The man was Nikesh, his mother was Sakshi, and the other son Sukesh was trying to push the wheelchair so that Nikesh could get blessings of the goddess.

Mallika had planned to go to Ellora caves later that afternoon, but when the family invited her for lunch, she quickly changed her plans. Sakshi talked about her family and asked Mallika about hers. She didn't know why, but Mallika told Sakshi the whole truth. After listening to Mallika, Sakshi suggested she give up her hotel room and come and stay with them. Mallika was reluctant, but Sakshi's warmth and love gave her comfort, and she felt sure she was in good hands. She became part of the family and took her turn at taking care of Nikesh. Sukesh was a math teacher in a local primary school, and little group was known to be a decent middle-class family. Mallika started dancing again, at first only to keep herself busy, but as time went on she became more and more passionate. Before long she decided to dedicate herself to learning and improving her ability.

Sakshi helped her find a teacher and a job in a local NGO. Mallika realized that she wanted to dance more than anything else, and for six years she gave herself over to her passion. Mallika thought of her mother and compared her to Sakshi. Her mother only wanted her to get married, not to pursue dance or even journalism. And now here was Sakshi, who encouraged her to follow her heart.

Sakshi's house was a home, albeit a tiny one. There were two rooms, one was a kitchen cum dining room cum storeroom. A small corner in the kitchen was converted into a washroom. The outside room was living room cum bedroom for this five-person family. They all started their day at 4 a.m. Sakshi worked as a caretaker in different homes, cleaning, polishing and in some homes even cooking and baking. Her husband worked at a grocery store. Sukesh had another year to finish before he got his doctorate in mathematics. They all hoped that he would be able to get a job as a professor in the local university. Each family member had assigned chores to keep the household running, and they all helped care for Nikesh. Mallika kept up with her dance practice and helped Sakshi by doing her chores and taking care of Nikesh. Sakshi encouraged Mallika to dance, for she knew how important it was to her.

Sakshi wanted Mallika and Sukesh to get married, but Mallika didn't know how to handle her past. She had left her husband and two children while they were sleeping. Sakshi asked Mallika for her old address and went to see Anand. At first he became upset and ordered her out of his house. Sakshi had relatives in that part of the city, so she stayed with them overnight and next morning went to Anand's with breakfast and some sweets. He talked with her and told her how devastated he was.

He was managing to raise the kids with Mallika's mother helping him. It was a great burden and in the three years since Mallika had left, Anand had let them think their mother had died. 'I had no clue where she was or how she was. I thought maybe she was dead,' Anand said.

Sakshi nodded and continued talking with Anand. Finally she told him she wanted Mallika and Sukesh to get married and that she believed Mallika was now ready set up a new life with her son. Anand was unsure at first, but after a few weeks he agreed to divorce Mallika. It took over a year for with the divorce to be final, and then Mallika and Sukesh were married in the presence of Sakshi, Nikesh and the priest who performed the ceremony.

In a few years, Mallika had her own students. She choreographed a dance for one of them for a school function. The student won first prize and Mallika was called up to share the stage with the winner. Word spread about her choreography, and Mallika was asked if she could give public performances.

Mallika realized she needed her teacher to start working with her again. He was more than willing, and she put her heart and soul into her practice. In a year's time she was winning local accolades for her performances. Slowly and steadily, Mallika managed to establish herself as a dancer who was serious about her work and her art. All the while her family supported and encouraged her.

Besides her dance, now there was another new love in her life: she had a baby girl. Sakshi stopped working and was soon widowed. The family had managed to save some money. Sukesh was earning a decent amount, and Mallika's performances brought in money as well. The family now could afford a decent home for them all, and after a while even Anand and the twins came to live with them.

***

Maya: So did you find my story interesting?

Day: Maya, what exactly are Mallika's feelings every time she decides one man or another isn't right for her, or the set up isn't to her liking? Isn't marriage supposed to be for richer and for poorer, in sickness and in health and all that? Mallika runs away every time, vows or no vows. She needs to be sure of what she wants so she doesn't damage other people's lives. Oh well, what can I say? I'm not supposed to judge.

Maya: We're not judging, we're just telling stories about how some women live their lives. We're observers. We might like some women and dislike others, but we're not living in their stories, so we get to do that. Are you ready for the next tale?

Day: Yes, but it can wait till tomorrow. I'm tired and sleepy now. Good night.

Chapter 17

Day: All right, Maya, let's see what you have this time.

Maya: I have some friendship tales, about women only.

Day: So far all your stories are about women. How is this one different?

Maya: You be the judge.

Just us

An actress, her maid and her mother are talking.

Mother: Okay, it's time to pack. What shall we do after that. I'm in no mood to go back to my old man. I know he'll be drunk. You know, I'm sure he's humping that office boy.

Actress: Ma, take it easy. Dad wasn't always like that.

Mother: Oh, so he started liking the company of young men overnight? What world are you living in, girl? This isn't the movies, it's real life.

Actress: Yeah Mom, you're right. You must be feeling so terrible. After all, you've been keeping up the pretense and living a lie for my sake, for the whole Celebrity Mom thing.

Mother: Not just for you. After all, what were my options? My parents died, and I wasn't getting anywhere as an actress. Your father was my last hope, and I married him. He's been this way since the beginning, and he wanted an image of a family man. He'd never have survived in the industry if they knew this about him. There were rumors, but he was at the top of his game, and everybody ignored the rumors because they loved the money he made for them. It's old age and sickness that forced him into retirement. I was a perfect cover for him, and you know what? I always wanted someone to pour my heart out to, someone who understood how I really felt about being trapped in that golden tower. Yes, I travelled wherever I felt like. I had the best food and wine in the best hotels, and oh, the shopping. It was nice to have several houses, but I couldn't make a real home in any of them.

Actress: Ma, why didn't you leave him? Or is that a silly question to ask?

Mother: Of course it is. Who would keep me in the style I was used to? I was supposed to be his overseas distributor, even his partner. By the way, that dress designer, that third-class darzi, what a cheapskate! He was the real reason for that overseas distribution opening. All I did was sign papers. I was getting used to turning a blind eye to this guy and guy thing when I saw the news items popping up. There were these starlets he pretended to be in love with because 'he was being nagged by his wife,' and I don't know what all, I stopped paying attention. It was a game to feed the media with juicy gossip so that he could carry on with his little secret. Each time one of these stories appeared I was given a blank cheque, or diamonds or a ticket to any luxurious place I wanted to go.

There was one trip that changed everything for me. There was a little girl who had won a beauty pageant, and he got interested in her, just to flirt with for the sake of the media. He made me call a journalist and spill the details about him. I was to say I was terribly upset and that I was going to visit my rich aunt in Paris.

For that lie he gave me a very special gift: not just a ticket to Paris, but also an escort. He was handsome and came from a very poor family. His father worked at a factory as a mill hand. My escort, I can't name him because he's now a star, was working as a security guard. He approached your father for roles, and he asked the young man to do this favor for him … Why are you looking so surprised? Taraji, you know that story, why the shocked expression?

Maid: Nahi bai, you said we aren't supposed to talk about this to baby.

Actress: Ma, what's Taraji talking about?

Mother: Sangeeta, listen and you'll find out why. That trip wasn't just a jaunt. It was supposed to last for a year or more.

Actress: But why, Ma? Who was taking care of Dad and his business?

Mother: Remember I told you about our so-called fight and my leaving him? I had to stay in Paris with my escort for a reason.

Actress: What reason, ma?

Mother: You were the reason.

Actress: What are you saying, Ma? What do you mean?

Mother: Okay, here it is. You aren't your father's daughter, but my escort's daughter, the child of a famous star. He was 21 and I was 37. Your father made a big tamasha of how forgiving he was and that he wanted to take care of his wife's child. He told the press it didn't matter who the father was. And he just happened to mention how he had given me respect and a standing in the community even though I was from the lowest rung of society. I wish I had had the guts to speak out, to tell the world about his devious mind and his manipulation. So that's the truth, my dear girl. Hold it close to your heart, for that is your truth.

Actress: I can't believe it. And Taraji knew all the time? Mom, why didn't you tell me?

Mother: Maybe I just couldn't find the right moment.

Actress: Then why did you choose today?

Mother: I felt like sharing with you, softly, without bitterness or anger. I wanted to speak the truth to you and unburden my heart. Kyon Taraji, shall we go and have some fun this week, the three of us?

Maid: Sure, memsaab. Let's start with pani-puri, then we'll go to our adda and do our usual masti.

Actress: But where are we going?

Mother: You'll see. Here, wear this wig and take off your false eyelashes and lipstick. We can pretend in the bus that you're a Sangeeta look alike.

The three boarded a bus and an hour later reached a village. After leaving the bus, they walked

about two kilometers to a mud and brick house. Taraji unlocked the door and they entered the cozy, tidy dwelling. Sangeeta had seen such homes on movie sets, but not in real life. Taraji brought her cool water in an earthen pot. The water was fragrant and tasty, fresh from a sparkling stream. Tea was served in dainty red clay cups.

Sangeeta indulged herself, lazily solving crossword puzzles until her attention was distracted by the aroma of curry and rotis. She realized that Taraji and Anusree were cooking on an open stove, with real wood and a sigri made of an unused bucket and lit with charcoal. Her mother, the stage mom, was actually baking rotis on that sigri. Sangeeta was finally able to relax, to take a vacation from her career, doing something simple instead of taking a fancy trip to an international destination. The aroma of the food made her hungry and she called out to her mother and Taraji.

Mother: Sangu, just few more minutes and we'll have dinner. Taraji, have you brought the things we need?

Taraji brought served dinner on humble aluminium plates. From a canvas bag, Taraji took a bottle of liquid that looked like water and three glasses.

Mother: Sangu, try this; it's better than your champagne.

The beverage was light and sweet, but its mild flavor was deceptive. The young woman began to feel lightheaded, and as she ate, she told her mother that food never tasted so good. Sangeeta the actress finally seemed to be having fun.

After dinner all three women dozed off. They slept all night and woke fresh as daisies in the morning. but getting up on that first morning, Sangeeta became upset. She wasn't prepared to bathe in a bucket using water from a small sink. Not only that, but there was an open toilet. Anushree calmed her daughter and urged her to get used to it, for they'd be here only another day or so. Sangeeta agreed, saying she'd be all right for such a short time.

Actress: So, Ma, this is your way of having masti? Is this what you meant by having fun? Well, let see … except for the toilet and bathing, I guess I am having fun.

They had breakfast and walked around the village. There wasn't much there, only a grocery store, a dairy, a vegetable vendor, and other small shops. There was a school, but the construction was crumbling. After an hour or so, Sangeeta and Anusree returned to the house with groceries for the day's cooking. Sangeeta checked her messages and went back to her puzzles, waiting for lunch. They had a spicy tender goat curry. She finished four rotis, proud that she was less lightheaded today.

Anusree was seeing her daughter as she was, carefree and away from the limelight. She wanted to capture these days in her memory and keep them for a lifetime. God alone knew when she would get such an opportunity again. Anusree was getting old, and she could not longer pretend to be what she was not. She was tired of being an overseas distributor of lucrative films and the wife of a famous producer-director. Besides that, in still a third public role, she was the mother of a very popular actress.

Everything was a sham. She had never had a chance at real life and she wanted that chance now. How could she make the change to an authentic life? Over tea, she shared her thoughts with her confidante Taraji, and the maid just smiled her usual smile. Anusree gazed at the neat little house and hoped that God would grant her wish to get away from that mad life she was leading.

It was their last evening in that house, and Taraji and Sangeeta decided to take a walk.

Maid: Baby, do you know how long your mother has been coming here?

Actress: No, how long

Maid: For almost five years. When she wanted to take a break when you were away on a shoot, she would come here. You mother is responsible for the school, and she is planning to build an ashram for the women of the town. There is no ashram yet, so they live in a temporary home that used to belong to a villager.

Actress: Taraji, who are these women, and why is my mother building an ashram for them?

Maid: They used to be film actors like you are today. Some worked as extras, some as dancers, and one famous star lives here. Her son and daughter were selfish, and when she was no longer in demand, she took to drinking and her family started to mistreat her. She ran from her home, and your mother brought her here. I'll tell you a secret, but first you have to promise me you won't tell anyone.

Actress: Okay, Baba, I promise.

Maid: The house where we're staying belongs to your mother. She also has a plot of land here.

Sangeeta felt very proud of her mother at that moment. Anusree could have taken refuge in toy-boys, or drinking and gambling, like so many others, but she was a noble person. Inspired by her mother, Sangeeta decided to make some changes in herself.

Sangeeta asked Taraji to take her to meet the women who were under her mother's care. Taraji was reluctant at first, but she obliged. With renewed vigor Sangeeta walked through the village with a fresh eye. When they reached the house, it looked old, with paint chipping off and a dull moist smell throughout. The only outward sign of life was a well-tended garden of vegetables and herbs.

Sangeeta entered and saw there were only a few rooms, but fifteen women lived in the house. She looked at each, searching for the aging movie star. When she saw her, Sangeeta realized the woman was still gorgeous. She was sweeping her room, head down, but her long black hair gave her away, along with her dark, clear complexion and a swanlike neck.

Maid: Baby, she is the famous Suryagandha. She went into a rage yesterday and broke a couple of things. That's why she's cleaning her room. Your mother has asked her to do some yoga. I hope it will do her some good.

Sangeeta didn't know how to react to this sad story, but she knew she was changing, deep down. She wanted things to be different; she wanted to make changes for the better. This trip had awakened something inside her. On the way back, Taraji noticed that her baby was a little preoccupied, and she smiled slightly.

They reached home and found Anusree packing for their trip home. The next day they went back to the city, and Sangeeta soon had to go to Amsterdam for a fortnight. During the flight, Sangeeta made a decision. She felt a connection to the older actress and believed they could form a bond of friendship. A week later, when Anusree came to see her in Amsterdam, Sangeeta poured out her heart. There had always been three of them: her mother, Taraji and herself. Now she felt as though a fourth woman had joined them. Sangeeta wanted to do something to turn her feeling into a reality.

Actress: Ma, I'd like to go back to the village with you and Taraji. I know about the good work you've been doing. I want to build that ashram for women and complete your half-built school. I want to learn, and then I want to help the children and the women manage their lives spiritually and live an independent life. Perhaps I could teach some acting skills I've picked up, the modern ones that the older women might not know.

Mother: Sangeeta, don't rush into anything. We mustn't decide such a serious matter in haste and later repent. You're used to a certain lifestyle; it might be difficult for you to give it all up.

Actress: No, Ma, I know what I want, I can sense it. If not now, I will still want to travel that route years from now. I know myself. I'm your daughter, and now I know what it means to be your daughter. But I will need you and Taraji with me.

They began making plans to go to the village. Sangeeta finished her projects in a few months, working hard and keeping her goal before her. Anusree made her own arrangements and told her husband about her plan. He wasn't willing to let go of her, but when she threatened to expose him to the public, he gave in. Taraji was always there for both of them. A few days before they made their move, Sangeeta made a request to her mother.

Actress: Ma, can you please tell me who my biological father is?

Mother: I guess it doesn't matter now. If you must know, he is Susheel Kumar—the actor who died last year in that car accident.

Actress: Now I know why you insisted that I had to pay my respects to him and his family. I thought it was because we were part of the fraternity. Ma, oh Ma, how I wish I had known it before. It would have been nice to be with him. We might even have become close.

Mother: You could never have done that. Trust me.

Actress: You seem to know what you're saying, Ma, so I'll try to let it rest.

Taraji's daughter joined the group and worked with them to develop the village, and the older actress became more her old self and helped out as well. In a few years' time, the ashram and the school were completed. Sangeeta was happy teaching children and spreading awareness about the truths of the modern world, even the less pleasant ones. Only knowledge would make it possible for these young people go out and help others, she knew.

Sangeeta had made friends outside the industry as well, including some university professors who willingly came over and helped out. Doctors came on a regular basis and provided free services in the town. More people came, and the community grew, with more people helping as more people came who needed help.

The old people's home played a vital part in developing the model village, and they started a small-scale industry crafting handmade goods, especially quilts, for which there was a great demand.

Then a few people doing social service in the village wanted Sangeeta to stand for election, but she was happy doing what she wanted to do. She said she had seen enough of public life, and Anusree answered the call. She was made an MP, and Taraji's work doubled. Sangeeta, Anusree, Taraji, her two daughters, and that old actress had begun something that gave people hope and provided a model for others who wanted to change the world.

Chapter 18

Day: Maya, let's go to some some nice place.

Maya: What? I'm broke and you want to go to a nice place? My project is over at work, and I'm sure my boss is planning to let me go. Don't work for anyone else, Puggu. You should try to create your own job. I'm good for nothing, I know. All I can do is daydream and talk with you.

Day: Okay, okay, there's no need to get upset. I meant in the story you tell—let's go to someplace nice.

Maya: Oh. Okay, I see what you mean. Let's see … I have one.

A Recession Story

The sign on the hair salon read: *Seeking healthy long hair, dark black color only please.*

Paroma had been walking since morning. She was about to quit her job hunt for the day and go home when the words caught her attention.

She was an elegant 25-year-old woman who had come to Canada from Kolkota in search of a better life with her husband, Gautam, who had lived in Canada for ten years. Paroma had just married him and moved here. He was an accountant with an international firm, and he had bought a big house with swimming pool, a car and all the things that make for a good life. He thanked God for his good fortune, not taking it for granted. Paroma left no stoned unturned in managing the house. It had three levels, with four bedrooms and three bathrooms. The basement had a screening room where they watched movies with their friends, as well as a comfortable den, wired for stereo, that looked out on the pool.

During the day, Paroma listened to her favorite Rabindra Sangeet music while relaxing with tea and her favorite tea biscuits. Sometimes, sitting in the den, she planned her paner pakoris and the chutneys for dinner on weekends. She would gaze at the pool and wait for summer to come, for Gautam had taught her to swim. Dreaming at times, laughing and singing, and taking a trip down memory lane, Paroma passed much of her time in the basement. Yes, she cleaned and dusted throughout the house, but she loved cleaning the basement because she entertained herself at the same time.

In the kitchen she played western music, which she was beginning to like. She sang and kept herself busy while cooking elaborate dinners for Gautam. This took up most of her time, in the planning as well as the preparation and the cooking. Fish was a staple, and she liked to cook with cottage cheese. Rice and rotis were a must, and if she was in a good mood, she fried pakoras for dinner. Their evening meal was usually a three course dinner complete with a homemade dessert.

Paroma held a masters in music from Kolkata university. She loved to read, she knew how to sew and embroider, and she would hum and sing all day. She had even made the beautiful quilt they had in their bedroom. She was planning to buy material for curtains and embroider them, but first she decided to take a walk and go grocery shopping. It occurred to her that Gautam had become busy at work and had not taken her out for two days. It was a routine: every Thursday they went grocery shopping and then to their favorite south Indian dosa place, where they ate to their heart's content. They started with appetizers like curd vada, idlys followed by dosas filled with potatoes, and they drank cold yoghurt drink with everything.

She realized they hadn't been to their favorite restaurant for over three weeks. Paroma decided to remind Gautam later, but first she needed her groceries. After she finished shopping, she called Gautam on his cell, but he didn't pick up. She tried his direct line at work, but no luck. She decided to cook plain dal and make do with some vegetables. With limited groceries, only what she could carry, it was impossible to create an elaborate dinner. Poor Gautam, she said to herself. He'll come home tired from work and will have to eat such simple food.

Gautam returned early from work and looked a bit down. Paroma quickly got him his tea and some biscuits. Gautam gave her a concerned look and she smiled back. Looking at her, Gautam decided it was high time he told her the truth. More than a month before, Gautam had lost his job. He had tried hard to get part-time work as an accountant, but because of the downturn, no one was hiring. Instead, people were closing down businesses.

Somehow Gautam managed to get work in a restaurant as a cashier, but it was a two-week temporary position until the cashier returned. Today he had collected his wages from the restaurant and the job was over. Gautam had been promised a couple of freelance jobs; his old company said there were projects coming up and he would be hired back. But when? He didn't know. How would he manage the life he had built, and even some of the basic necessities? A garage sale was at the top of his list, but they needed a lot more than that.

He broke the news gently to Paroma. She was naïve; she lived in a dream world. He didn't want her to be exposed to this harsh reality. He loved her, and he wanted to take care of her and be her provider, but now it looked like it wasn't going to happen. He had to tell her; he had no choice.

'Paroma, I want to tell you something very serious,' Gautam began.

Paroma knew this had to happen. She was no longer the beauty he had married in Kolkata. Her sarees and her jewelry were all packed away. She hardly ever got a chance to get dressed in her fine clothes and tie her long lustrous tresses with bejeweled clips. After being married for 18 months, Gautam had found someone else, she thought, and her life was over. Her dream of loving Gautam and having children had crashed.

But Gautam was trying his best to explain how they would have to plan their expenses and how he would train her to live within a limited budget. This way, he said, they could survive a few more months, but he admitted he should have saved a little more for a rainy day.

Paroma broke away from her thoughts, and it took her a minute to realize what her husband was talking about. It hit her that he had lost his job and that things were about to change. She listened and agreed to do whatever Gautam said was necessary. She loved him very much and would do anything for him. Paroma made her own to-do list and went about looking for jobs. Paroma had no experience to speak of; all she knew was how to make delicious meals and keep a home for Gautam.

Days went by and turned into weeks. They held tightly to whatever was left after paying their bills, but that was less and less each month. Thus one day during her walk through town, Paroma saw the sign asking for long, black, healthy hair, and the salon was ready to pay $100. She entered confidently and asked for the manager. She was a kind lady, and she smiled at Paroma and paid her $200.

Paroma went home happy, hugging her grocery bag filled with all the essentials she would need to cook Gautam's favorite dishes. It had been a while since she had cooked a decent meal for the love of her life.

Chapter 19

Day: So how's work? I like your stories to much I almost forgot you have to work too.

Maya: The job is fine, I love my work. Oh, I didn't get fired after all. But sometimes it's frustrating, too. I'm feeling kind of weak and tired. My asthma is troubling me, and there's still a nagging ache in my wisdom tooth.

Day: But Maya, those are chronic, and they'll wear you down. What have you done about them? Have you gone to the doctor? Do you *ever* keep a doctor's appointment. I think you have some kind of medical phobia.

Maya: No, that's not it. There are just a few things that are stressful. My driver's license has expired and I hate not driving. But the test for the license costs money, and I need to cut expenses so I can pay for it. I'm trying, Puggu. Okay, I'm off to make some vegetable curry and rice. I'll be in the kitchen; come on in and make yourself comfortable.

Day: You said on the phone the other day that Mom was sick. How is she?

Maya: Well, Puggo, you know it's serious, she has survived two heart attacks and she may even be gone. I'm afraid to call my parents. Let's see, here's a nice bottle of wine. I don't want to deal with this now. I'm so hungry; I guess I haven't been making very good dinners for myself. I'm living on what I eat at work, I guess. But I want to cook my own food—curry and spice and everything nice. What do you say? Hmmm, you look bored. Good night, Puggu.

Early the next morning, the phone rings.

Day: Maya, your phone was ringing, but it stopped. I see the light blinking; there's a message. Go check your messages, Maya.

Maya: Puggu, I don't want to. I'm afraid. Besides, if she dies I'll know it right away.

Day: That's rubbish. She could have turned the corner, she could be almost well by now.

Maya: No, really, I sense these things. I would know. Let me tell you a tale of love.

Love Just Happens

Pratap was married, and so was Padma. But Padma fell in love; she even believed that Pratap was the man for her.

Sipping tea, Padma tried to deal with this new development. After finishing her tea, she washed the mug in the kitchen sink and left it on the rack. She walked the few steps to the large window in her kitchen and started thinking.

'How shall I let him know that I love him? What if he thinks of me as a person with no character? After all, I'm a married woman with children, and Sanjay is a major part of my life.'

Padma started wondering if Sanjay loved her enough. Yes, he did, in his own way. Did she love him? She received no reply from the little voice inside her head. By then her children were back from school, and Padma got busy serving their lunch.

Sanjay came home from work and took and their family of six—they had two daughters and two sons—out for dinner. Sanjay wanted a change, Sandhya and Sanjna were bored with Padma's cooking, and Arun and Ajit were okay with anything as long as they could bring their video games and play without having to take part in the conversation.

Days turned into weeks, and Padma started feeling alone and distant in her marriage. Sanjay was just Sanjay. He did all that he had been doing for the past seventeen years. He went to work, took the family out for lunch and dinners, helped with the chores, and went to parent teacher meetings. Padma was happy; she couldn't ask for more from Sanjay. But there was something about Pratap.

Who was Pratap? To Padma, he was the person she loved the most. She felt a little funny about this, for she didn't know him that well, but interacting with him daily at the library where they both volunteered, she sensed that he was a real person. She felt a connection with him and her heart raced, not just from lust, but from real love. Padma knew her feelings for Pratap couldn't be anything but love. She needed to explore her feelings and share them with him. but how? They both were married.

One day on her way to work, Padma decided to tell Pratap how she felt about him, and that she would love him no matter what. All she wanted was for Pratap to know how she felt about him. She was ready to face the consequences. She told herself she was prepared to allow Pratap to think whatever he wanted to. She soon did as she had prepared herself to do: she declared her love for him. Pratap was taken aback, and nothing happened right away. Life went on as before for them both.

They went to work and came home, they loved their families and everything seemed normal on the surface. But because Padma had opened her heart to Pratap, life could not simply go on, at least not for her. She wanted nothing short of his whole presence in her life. She wanted Pratap for herself; she wanted to care for him, to love him and keep him with her. She understood the situation, and yet she demanded more from him.

Soon after Padma revealed her feelings for him, Pratap offered his shoulder as a friend, with set limits to the friendship. But love knows no boundaries—it just happens. Padma forgot herself, forgot the limits. All she could see was Pratap and how he should be with her.

Padma, the docile, sensitive person, transformed into a jealous, calculating woman. She knew only one thing, that Pratap belonged to her. A meeting with Pratap wasn't just coffee and smiles, as it was supposed to be. Those open chats that took account of their situation vanished into thin air, and, truth be told, Pratap was becoming fond of her. But Padma couldn't see that. She wanted a deep understanding where hearts met and merged. Soon she lost herself and focused on one thing: either destroy him or destroy herself. She wanted an end to it, one way or the other.

At first, Pratap wanted to be kind to her, to offer friendship, but then came the wrath of the woman in love. Padma decided to kill herself, leaving a note stating the reason. Sanjay was leaving for a short trip with their sons, and the daughters were visiting their grandparents. Padma pleaded a heavy workload and didn't accompany any of them.

It was late evening. Padma had bought a bottle of wine, and she had hidden a great many sleeping pills. She turned on the television and was ready to commit suicide within the hour. The wine made her drowsy, and she was taking the sleeping pills two at a time. Her perception dimmed; she could sense only her love for Pratap. It was as if she were moving into a narrow space where there was only her strong love. In this space, everything about Pratap became clearer. Those sweet moments with him, the bond he created with her, were alive in some corner of his heart. In this place his love for her grew and blossomed, hidden from the world, the world that was tearing her apart. This was the foundation for their love, that it dwelt in their hearts and not in external expressions like home, family, or external events. It was a merging of mind and heart, but not of body.

And then Padma jumped up, made a pot of strong coffee and destroyed the letter. After a few hours, she came to her senses. She needed to love Pratap for what he was, not for what she wanted him to be. She no longer felt like the other woman; she just felt like his woman. He was her man, no matter what, and she knew he loved her in the same way. There was a love that they could share. It wasn't the traditional kind, but it was a real love, and that was enough.

Day: So how does it end? What happens?

Maya: Puggu, in love there are no endings, happy or otherwise.

Chapter 20

Day: Maya, wake up, it's snowing. The whole world is white and beautiful. And you have to shovel the driveway.

Maya: Why do you have to startle me awake? I know I have to shovel the driveway. Yes, of course, it will give me much-needed exercise. Where's that 'white and beautiful world' you were talking about? Maybe it will motivate me.

Maya gets dressed in her boots, sweater, parka, scarf, and gloves and looks for the snow shovel. Later, she comes back and starts taking everything off, dripping melted snow on the rug.

Day: Maya is everything okay with you?

Maya: Sure, why do you ask?

Day: It's been a while since you've told me a story.

Maya: You know, while I was shoveling I was thinking the same thing. I have a story about Rose, that cute little child star. Move over, I'm freezing.

Lights, Action, and Tears

I loved watching movies. I never had money to buy tickets, for my parents were only thinking of survival. There was money for food, but not enough for a decent home or even basic education for me, and I was not alone. My parents had more mouths to feed besides mine, for we were a family of six. Whenever I felt hungry, I would go to the cinema hall and look at the posters. With all those superstars gazing at me, I forgot my hunger and lost myself in their world of dreams and hope.

Oh, by the way, my name is Jasmine and I am 8 years old. The reason I can enter the cinema hall is that I am responsible for bringing milk to the watchman, who lives in a little corner of the hall. I get paid Rs 100 per month. One of these days I'll use some of that money to buy a ticket and sit on a cushioned seat to watch a movie. I'm tired of watching from edges and corners and half open doors, of sitting on the steps beside the row of seats. For now it's a dream, but one day it will turn real. Oh, I have to leave the hall, it's time to help Mother wash the clothes.

Thus talking to herself, Jasmine reached their tiny house and a minute later came out with a bundle balanced on her head. Her mother wasn't finished getting ready, but Jasmine didn't want to stay indoors, for she didn't like the small room filled with people. As she set out with the bundle, she was approached by a man wearing a straw hat and dark glasses. Jasmine yelled for help, and her mother rushed to her rescue. The man in the sunglasses was taken aback. He apologized to her mother and introduced himself as Shankarrao, the famous filmmaker.

The mother had heard of him, but Jasmine knew his movies and started rattling off their names. Shankarrao was amazed by her memory and told the mother that he wanted to cast Jasmine in his next film. He added that he had auditioned many children and none filled the bill. Finally, his friend the cinema owner mentioned the little girl who supplied milk to the watchman. He had seen this little girl staring at the posters and losing herself completely in them. The owner said he was intrigued by the child's devotion to the movies. He had been watching her for almost a year now. He knew she was in love with cinema and thought she might be the girl the filmmaker was looking for. When the filmmaker came to visit, he didn't imagine he would create so much commotion.

Jasmine was suited to the role, and she was a natural in front of the camera. Three months later the shooting was over and now the family had some money. A couple of magazine interviews had made Jasmine a known face, and there were a few offers to endorse products. The parents were willing to spare her for a few thousands.

A well-wisher said that the way to succeed was to hire an agent and get organized. An agent, he said, would be able to get the market rate for her endorsements. Not only that, he would help her get work. They need not look for jobs; their daughter was a star, and work should come to her. They thought they could just close their eyes and an agent would be there, standing in front of them. And yes, they wished, and quickly they found a willing agent.

Jasmine started her day planning her schedule with her agent. It was a daily grind of endorsements, interviews, auditions, previews. For those, she got to sit on sofas and watch movies. One day in the preview theatre, she suddenly remembered she had forgotten to say good-bye to her first employer, the watchman. She made a mental note to do that the next day.

Jasmine didn't realise that, while enjoying all previews and becoming friends with 'auntys and uncles' from the media and the industry, she had no control over anything. Her days were not hers, her time was paid for, so it couldn't be used for her own purposes.

Jasmine wanted to get away from all this and run free for a few hours. She planned to sneak out while her parents and her agent were having a meeting over lunch. Jasmine tiptoed out of the house, still wearing her expensive dress. She didn't realise how much things had changed; to her the lanes she walked were the same. But now Jasmine and her family lived in a bigger house near their old tiny place. In the new house, she had a room to herself and could pick up the intercom and ask for a meal, a glass of juice, or anything else she wanted.

Jasmine thought back to the day that Shankarrao had scared her out of her wits. Soon after that, they had started shooting, and a month later her family moved out of the little home she was born in. She saw her old pal Bharti and called out to her, but Bharti didn't acknowledge her greeting, and Jasmine wondered why. She was too young to understand that stardom means isolation. Creating a dream world for others involves the harsh reality of getting ready for a scene, working with different costars, going from one set to another, giving interviews, putting up a friendly public face, and so many other things that actors don't have time to create dreams for themselves.

Jasmine had gone from dreaming and losing herself in those posters to weaving illusions that created a dream world for others. She saw the watchman and ran to him. After apologies and a home. She said good-bye to the watchman and promised to come and see him another day.

As soon as she stepped inside, she felt a stinging sensation on her cheek. It took a second for Jasmine to see that her father had slapped her. She wasn't even given time to recover. She was pushed into a room filled with media, producers, and fans, but before that she heard her father say 'Better keep that smile on, and don't you dare mention the slap.' Jasmine was a born actress, so it was easy for her to do as she was directed. But something inside her died. It was the hope that she could live her life as she wished, with dreams and freedom.

***

Maya: Puggu, today I'm not telling a story about another woman. I'll read you a poem I wrote for myself.

Day: So, no more tales?

Maya: I'm not sure. But I deserve a story of my own, in verse.

When life gets complicated, try simple things.

Sing a song

Watch a movie
Gaze at the sky
Use humor and laugh.

Just stay calm and still
Solutions will appear
Do not think
Staying quiet
Physically and mentally
You are recharging your mind
Your mind needs rest
There is too much chattering inside.
Just be quiet.
Women, you need to
Stay calm and collected
For only then
can you realize your strength.